TWING

The Heir of Magic and Moonlight

DANIELLE HILL

www.daniellehillwrites.ca

Trigger and content warnings include: Abuse (mentions of physical and mental), alcoholism and alcohol consumption, anxiety, blood, death, demons, grievance/loss, murder, profanity, sexuality (mentions/non explicit), suicide & self sacrifice, and violence.

Cover Design: Celingraphics

Logo Design: rebecacovers

ISBN: 978-1-7779909-1-6

To my amazing mom. Thank you for everything you've done, and everything you continue to do.

Estrella

Caelia

Nix

Kingdom of Soluna

Safe House

Shadow Lands

Kingdom of Coldoria

CAELESTIA

GLOSSARY

Word and name pronunciations:

Amara: ah-mar-ah

Avery: eh-ver-ree

Benjamin: Ben-juh-min

Caelestia: kah-lest-ee-ah

Caelia: Kah-lia

Calypso: Kah-lip-so

Chaz: Ch-azz

Coldoria: Cold-or-ee-ah

Cyra: K-eye-rah

Erik: Air-ick

Esmeray: Ez-mer-eye

Estrella: S-tray-ah

Hazel: Haze-ul

Lawrence: Lore-ance

Lola: Low-la

Meresay: Mare-say

Soluna: Sole-loo-nah

Ophiuchus: Oh-few-kiss

Orion: Oh-ryan

Xander: Zand-er

A Kingdom of Sun and Shadow Recap

Once upon a time, Avery led a normal existence in the mortal world, but then one night, she was transported to another world. Avery discovered she had a twin sister she never knew existed, Amara, who turned out to be the heir to his Kingdom she was now in.

Amara had known of Avery's existence for a short period of time before she brought Avery to the kingdom of Soluna. Amara also knew that she needed to find the prophecy that would prove she was fit to rule her kingdom, so she ventured off with her best friend, and royal guard, Wesley to find this prophecy. Leaving Avery behind to impersonate a sister and life she knew nothing about.

While Avery was impersonating Amara, she met her fiancé, Xander. She later realized it had been an arranged engagement and that Amara and Xander hated one another.

Avery and Xander were forced to spend time in each others company while he was staying in Soluna and they ended up calling a truce, eventually becoming somewhat friends.

Avery soon discovered that she had the ability to hear the thoughts of those around her. She had never experienced anything like it before she arrived in Soluna.

Avery and Amara both had nightmares about a person cloaked in shadows and darkness who called themselves Shadow Lord.

Amara eventually made it to the safehouse with Wesley where they searched for any information about a prophecy they could find. Eventually, Amara found tunnels located beneath the safehouse which led them to an underground temple that had sun and moon markings along the floors.

Amara reached for the alter in the centre of the room and it lit up before she was shown a vision of the past.

500 years ago lived another set of twins, Calypso and Cyra. They had powers no one had even seen before and the people of their villagers hated and hunted them for it. After Cyra was killed, Calypso had been given Cyra's powers along with immortality and the power of creation. Calypso gifted a selected few their own powers, and called them Celestials.

Calypso's powers were too strong and she could not control them. Eventually, they became too much and part of her split, creating a shadow-self who called herself Esmeray.

Avery went to Coldoria for the Winter Moon Festival, along with most of the inhabitants of Soluna. Once there, she learned even more about Xander and his family.

Before the first night of the festival began Avery was knocked unconscious and woke up in a dungeon where she was attacked by a shadow demon.

Ben had found and saved Avery, bringing her back to her room. Xander found out about the attack and went back to Soluna, leaving the festival early, where they believed it to be safe.

Amara and Wesley found themselves in the Shadow Lands, a place ruled by the Shadow Lord. Many other celestials lived there but hid in fear of the Shadow Lord finding them and taking their powers for themself.

A barrier surrounded the Shadow Lands keeping all those inside of it trapped.

Calypso spoke to Amara and told her that only she could pass safely through the barrier before she gave Amara the prophecy she'd been searching for.

Demons, unlike the shadow ones they had faced before, attacked. Wesley pushed Amara through the barrier to escape and save herself as well as her kingdom.

While Avery and Xander snuck out of the castle to go out for dinner, they realized they were being followed. They ran to escape Hazel and Ben as they spied on the two. While hiding in an alley they were attacked by more demons.

Once they were back at the castle, Avery finally went to Lawrence for more answers as to what was happening and her past. Lawrence confessed that Soluna had once been full of people with different magical abilities and magic itself.

Years ago, Calypso had spoke to the then Queen in her dreams, that Avery and Amara were the chosen ones and to protect Avery they had to send her away.

They hid Avery in the mortal world and demons attacked. Killing the King and Queen and wiping the minds of everyone who did not posses magic in the kingdom of the existence of magic and celestials.

Because of Calypso's warning to the Queen, Lawrence had been giving the only protection potion to save him and his memories of magic and their people. He is the only one to know of magic and celestials.

After all the new information Avery had been given, she needs to think and on her walk through the corridors she is attacked by demons yet again.

Xander finds her and saves her. She wants to confess that she is not who he thinks she is, but he says he already knows.

Amara is finally back at the castle and fills Lawrence in on everything that had happened while she was gone and the prophecy. While they are talking in his office they hear Avery scream and run to find her.

They find her with Xander, unconscious.

PROLOGUE

Xander

It had only been a couple of days since I'd last seen Amara, since the encounter with those demonic creatures in that dark alley. I couldn't stop thinking about the look in her eyes just before we said our goodbyes for the night; couldn't forget the true fear and instinctive protectiveness that had infiltrated my body and seemed to linger long after the threat had vanished.

So earlier in the day, when Erik had brought up the prospect of a night out, I had practically lunged for the door, more than keen on the idea of distracting myself from my endless ruminations about jewel-toned eyes and shadow demons.

Walking down one of the castle corridors with Erik and Vic in tow, we headed towards the back entrance that led toward the direction of town. Beyond grabbing a few drinks and something to eat, we hadn't discussed any specific plans for the night, other than finding some sort of entertainment to breathe some life back into us, some fun to break up the monotony.

Vic droned on and on about some interaction she had with one of the other Ladies that had been visiting, and naturally, Erik kept pressing her for more and more information about that particular Lady. I rolled my eyes at their theatrics as I tried to stifle my grin. There was comfort in the fact that these two never seemed to change, unlike *some* people around here. *Some people* with eyes the color of—

A flash of honey blonde interrupted my vision, pulling me out of my train of thought as I rounded the corner and smacked right into another body with an audible, *"Oof."* My hands shot out on instinct, landing on delicate shoulders in an effort to steady the other and bringing me face to face with none other than Amara herself… as if I had somehow willed her to me via my own thoughts.

I was momentarily lost for words but thankfully did eventually find my tongue.

"Amara, my apologies. I— I didn't see, didn't hear you coming. Wasn't paying attention. Are you okay?" I smiled, not even trying to hide how pleased I was to see her, my hands still wrapped gently around each of her upper arms.

Those eyes narrowed as they met my gaze and within half a breath, her arms were ripped from my grasp. Taking a quick step back from me, Amara pushed her arms out in front of her, forcing space between us before shaking her head and continuing right past me, my ears barely picking up the sound of her muttering something underneath her breath as she did so.

Caught off guard by her behavior, it took me a second before I pulled myself together and turned to call out to her just as she reached the end of the corridor. "Hey! Amara, wait up!"

She froze before slowly pivoting back to face me.

I held her gaze, curiosity spearing me as I spoke to the others, assuring them that I'd meet them downstairs. Unphased by my run-in and still deep in discussion over that same Lady in question, they wandered off as I closed the space between myself and Amara.

"Have you been avoiding me?" I teased, trying to lighten the mood as a playful smirk tugged at the corner of my lips.

Her gaze seemed to size me up before her lips parted on an answer. "It's more likely than not."

A laugh jolted out of me, but as I assessed her expression and found no warmth or amusement there, my smile fell. "Is everything all right?"

"It will be… once I can get back to what I was doing and further away from you, and whatever *this* is," she practically hissed, her words laced with venom. She didn't so much as wait for a response from me before turning on her heel, leaving me there frozen and speechless in her wake.

Where did that *come from?* I wondered, confusion making my brows furrow as I walked back to where Erik and Vic were waiting for me.

As we walked to the castle gate, I couldn't stop replaying our last two interactions in my head on a loop. The last time I'd seen Amara before tonight was when we went out for dinner together. And sure, the night certainly didn't end on a good note, but I couldn't quite figure out what *I* did to deserve that ice-cold response. It wasn't an actual date, so it wasn't as if she expected me to reach out… right?

I wracked my brain as I tried to make sense of it. In the past, I probably would have just chalked it up to Amara being Amara, but if I was being honest with myself, that wasn't possible anymore. So many things were changing between us recently, and I had no interest in things going back to the way they used to be. This little cold slap of apathy from her was enough for me to be sure of that.

I should go find her. I should do the mature thing and try to talk to her. Figure this out.

"Hellooo? Caelestia to Xander!? I swear your mind is always somewhere else these days," Victoria whined, rolling her eyes dramatically. Erik just chuckled knowingly as if he knew my next move before I made it.

"Uh, sorry. You know what? I forgot... that I can't actually go out. Yeah. You two go, have enough fun to make up for my absence." Before they could get a word out to object, I flashed them a toothy smile and dashed back the way I came.

I immediately headed toward Amara's room, which seemed like the obvious spot to start my hunt for her. When I eventually arrived just outside her door, I took a few deep breaths and tried my best to collect my thoughts even as my brain felt empty of any real strategy. *Come on, Xander. Think of something.*

I reached out to rap my knuckles against the wood, accidentally nudging the door open slightly before my knuckles could make contact a second time. Cocking my head as a frown tugged my brows inward, I gently pushed the door open further. The room itself was pitch black save for the small flicker of a flame on the far side of the room that was just bright enough to outline the slight figure nearby.

Amara hadn't noticed me yet as I took a couple of steps into the room, my eyes still adjusting to the darkness. She

19

was hunched over the nightstand by the bed, rooting through the drawers.

"Amara?" I practically whispered in an attempt not to scare her and make her even more upset with me.

She jumped to her feet and spun around to face me, her surprise sending something dropping to the floor with a small thud. I winced, guilt flooding me as I rushed over to help pick up whatever she had dropped, my fingers quickly coming into contact with what felt like a leather binding.

"I'm so sorry, I didn't mean to—" The flickering candlelight brought my gaze up and up, straight into the eyes of... *not* Princess Amara at all. I jolted back, suspicion flaring over my features as I took in the man before me.

The Duke of Caelia.

"What are you doing in here?" he sneered, his hands aimlessly searching the floor for the item he had dropped— the item that was now firmly grasped in one of my hands, pressed against my back as I rose to my feet.

"I could ask you the same thing. Last I checked, this *isn't* your room." My eyes narrowed as I waited for an explanation, fingers deftly sliding the item into a pocket and away from his reach.

The Duke scrambled to his feet, clearly feigning shock and embarrassment. "Oh, my! Would you look at that? You are right. Silly me. I'll just… be on my way now!" I nodded once, allowing him to rush from the room without another word.

Once he was long gone, I removed the item from my pocket, flipping it over in my hands. It was a small, leather-bound journal with a jagged piece of paper shoved deep into its pages, perhaps marking someone's place. Intrigue tugged at me, knowing it was something that belonged to Amara, but despite that curiosity, I knew it would be a gross invasion of privacy if I so much as cracked open the first page.

But the Duke wanted to possess it for a reason—apparently a reason strong enough to warrant breaking in and ransacking the Princess's room, so I had no intention of leaving it behind for him to sniff out again.

I tucked the journal away, securing Amara's door before resuming my search for her around the castle, mostly coming up empty. I needed to find her, needed to return her journal and inform her about my discovery of the Duke. Huffing under my breath as I wandered the corridors, I knew there was another reason why I needed to find Amara.

I just needed her to talk to me.

CHAPTER ONE

Avery

"Avery!" yelled a familiar voice, making my eyes fly open as the sound startled me from a restless sleep. My heart hammered in my chest as I tried to make heads or tails of where I was. "Avery! Answer me! Are you here?"

I jolted up to a seated position, my hand flying to shield my eyes from the intense light streaming through the windows and illuminating every corner of my bachelor apartment.

My apartment?

"Avery, this isn't funny. Open the door!" Lola continued to holler from the hallway, her fist pounding heavily on the door.

Moving to my feet, I took long strides to cross the room quickly and pulled the door open, if only to shut Lola up. Her arms were still raised when she appeared before me, poised for more knocking. A small noise left her throat as she practically jumped on me, wrapping her arms around my neck and hugging me tightly.

"Oh, thank God, you're alive!" she cried.

"What happened? How did I get here?" I asked, holding her at arm's length while my frantic eyes searched hers for answers.

"So much for not drinking last night. You're in worse shape than I am," she laughed as she pushed past me toward the kitchen.

I spun around to follow her, my arms waving in frustration and utter confusion. "No, seriously, how did I get here?"

"Seriously?" she asked, rifling through the cupboard and refrigerator before pulling out a bottle of vodka from the freezer and poured herself a drink. "You left super early last night. I assumed you just came back here. At least that's what your text said."

My brows tied together as I tried to understand. "Last night?"

"O-M-G! Yes, last night. We went to Sirens, and as usual, you bailed and texted that you were home safe. Blah blah blah," she trailed off into her glass before downing it in one gulp. She poured another drink and then continued, "But by the looks of things, you *didn't* go straight home." She tipped her glass in my direction, arching a brow in a silent question.

"What? What the hell are you talking about? That was over a month ago. I—I left. I went to a completely different world—"

Lola cut me off. "Are you alright? Maybe someone spiked your drink. Do you want me to take you to the hospital?"

"No! I think I just… need to sit down." Moving to the end of my bed, I did exactly that as she stared at me with suspicion.

I reached for my cell phone on my nightstand. The date was the 2nd of September. But that didn't make sense since I left for Soluna on the 1st. My brain was spinning with questions that I didn't have answers to. "Are you sure? I really think I should take you to get checked out. You keep spacing out. Did you hit your head on your way home?"

"No, I'm fine. Just… hungover. You should go," I stood to my feet and ushered Lola back toward the door. "Thank you for checking on me. I'll call you later, promise."

"Okay, but if you don't, I'm coming by again," she said as I practically slammed the door in her face.

"What is happening?" I looked around my tiny apartment for clues about what had happened and how I had gotten there. I paced the floor as I tried to piece it together step by step, tracing back in my memory to the day I left.

My mom! She told me to go with Lawrence. She's the one who said I could trust him.

I immediately grabbed my phone and called her, listening impatiently as the ringing resounded several times before going to voicemail. *Of course.* "Think, Avery," I muttered under my breath. *It was a Saturday. Where would she be on a Saturday?*

And just like that, my phone started ringing. The name that popped up on the screen had a relieved gasp escaping my lips.

"Mom! Oh, thank God."

"What's wrong, Avery? Is everything alright?"

"You tell me. How did I get back? Where are Lawrence and Amara?"

Where's Xander? My heart skipped a beat as his face appeared in my mind. Being with him was the last thing I remembered before waking up here.

"I'm sorry, honey, I have no idea what or who you're talking about. Have you been experimenting with drugs? I know you're going back to college and trying to figure out what you want to do with your life, but Avery, drugs are not it. I know the college exper—"

"What? No! I'm not on *drugs*, mom." *But I'm beginning to think the rest of the world is right now.* "You introduced me to Lawrence, mom. You told me to go with him. You're the one who told me to trust him."

"I did no such thing. Did some strange man tell you he knew me and that I said that? Avery, do not go with this

25

strange man, do not trust him. I'm coming over right now. Call the police—"

"No!" I cut her off mid-ramble. "No, don't call the police. Don't come over. I… I'm just kidding. Ha-ha. I have to go, mom. I'll call you later." I hung up just as I heard her yelling something into the phone.

None of this makes sense. I was there; I know *I was. So why does no one else seem to remember anything? I was gone for over a freaking month!*

Groaning, I flopped onto my bed, my head smacking against something hard. Scrunching up my face, I moved the covers down to reveal a book. '*The Lost Princess of Soluna.*' No, that didn't make any sense. It wasn't a book, and it wasn't a dream. It was real, and it *really* happened to me. I know it did.

One minute I was in Soluna fighting shadow demons, and the next, I woke up in bed as if no time had passed. But why?

The more I examined my room for clues about what was happening, the more confused I became. My room was mine, yes, but it was as if the details were off. The photos I had displayed were different, the books on my shelves were replaced with others, and as I stepped back and really looked at the room, I noted that the entire colour scheme was just slightly off.

Nothing was as I remembered it.

Walking to the other side of my apartment, I entered the bathroom and noted something similar. The lavender theme was gone, replaced with a slightly darker, richer shade of purple. I pressed my hand against my forehead and took a deep breath, perplexed. *Maybe I'm losing it.*

Hoping to clear my head, I decided on a quick shower. Sadly, the only thing I could think about the entire time was how wonderful Amara's shower had been. As I washed my hair and put on fresh clothes, I kept repeating to myself that it was real, that it hadn't been just a dream or a delusion.

When I finally picked up my phone again, I was surprised to see so many missed calls and messages from Lola and my mom. Ignoring them for the moment, I snatched up my purse, stuffed my phone and wallet inside, and walked out the door, hoping that a walk and some fresh air would help.

"It was real," I whispered while waiting for the elevator to get to my floor. I was restless, my mind still actively replaying everything that had happened. Once the doors opened, I stepped inside the empty space. After pushing the button for the lobby, I impatiently tapped my foot the entire way down.

Once the doors opened and I entered the lobby, I smiled at Mr. Anderson as I passed by the front desk. He greeted me with a nod, just like he always did. But something caught my attention enough to do a double-take. I noted how his eyes appeared hollow, as if he hadn't slept in weeks and how his usually clean-shaven face was hidden behind an unruly swathe of hair.

But I shrugged it off as I walked outside to the crowded street, knowing I had more important things to figure out than Mr. Anderson's shaving habits. Looking around, I couldn't help but notice that everything about the busy main street seemed off, too.

I decided to retrace the steps of my last night here, hoping it might help me figure out what was going on. The more I saw, the more confused I became. Everything around me was hazy, including my mind, like a fever dream I couldn't wake from.

Faces blurred, shops seemed to blend, and nothing looked or felt right. Solid brick walls replaced the windows I had watched my reflection in so many times. Two-story buildings were now too many to count at first glance. Some of my favourite shops didn't even seem to exist any longer.

An eerie whistle caught my attention like a siren's call, luring me closer even though I wasn't interested in following. The sound of my name appeared to be carried back to me by the wind. I'd watched enough horror movies to know to run in the opposite direction, and still, my body moved by forces beyond my control.

My body practically jerked to a halt right in front of an alleyway. The same alley where I had first seen that creepy creature. Deep in the shadows, I half expected to see two or more glowing red eyes staring back at me. It must have been my lucky day because I was met with nothing but darkness.

"Avery."

A soft whisper called out to me again. Spinning around, I was again met with nothing.

"Fuck this!" I shouted, finally able to move my own limbs. I hightailed it away from the alley as fast as my short legs would take me.

Once I made it to the park I cut through last night, I nearly collapsed. Hunched with my hands on my knees and head between my arms, I tried to catch my breath, feeling a stitch steadily forming in my side.

Finally able to breathe somewhat normally again, I straightened. Taking in the park around me, I quickly noticed how different everything looked.

The trees were replaced with pink cherry blossoms on one side, and the other side looked like its trees were decaying. People walked by, paying no attention to the dying trees as if it were completely normal. In the centre of the park was an enormous fountain, each tier cascading into the next until finally landing in a small pond.

You could barely even call this place a park before; it had been mostly just an empty lot with grass and a few benches. Now, every way my eyes wandered, I was met with lush landscaping and extravagant flower arrangements. It all seemed so unnecessary.

This isn't right. I told myself as I tried to envision what it was supposed to look like, but my mind came up short.

A ringing sounded in my mind like an alarm trying to warn me. But warn me of what? I couldn't piece together a single thought as my mind raced. I squeezed my eyes shut to try and concentrate. My fingers raked through my hair and gripped tightly, nearly pulling it out as I tried to figure out what I was forgetting.

The ringing in my head stopped when it was replaced by another muffled ringing noise sounding from my purse. I stopped, blinking several times before slowly removing my hands from my hair and rifling through my bag for my phone to look at the screen, not recognizing the number.

"Hello?" I said as I brought my phone to my ear.

"Miss Bate?" a male voice answered.

"Y-yes, That's me."

"Hello, Miss Bate. I am the Chancellor of Oakdale University. I have been trying to get a hold of you. It seems we had a problem with some of your tuition forms. We need you to come in and sign some paperwork before you start Monday."

"Oh, I'm so sorry. I will come in later today, if that works."

"Yes, the office closes early today as it is Saturday. Can you make it here within the hour?"

"I'll be there, yes, thank you."

"Of course, just head to the administration office when you arrive. Thank you."

Before I could reply, the line went dead, and I was left staring at my phone in my hand.

This must have been what I was forgetting.

CHAPTER TWO

Xander

"Avery!" A familiar voice shouted. Jolting up, the Lord Regent and Princess Amara ran toward me, but not the Princess Amara I had been holding in my arms. "Do not touch her!"

"What are you talking about? Was I supposed to just let her fall to the ground? I caught her; I didn't *push* her." My eyes rolled as I slowly lowered her gently to the ground. "What happened to her?" I asked, looking down to assess her as she lay there unmoving. "Those things attacked us again. Is she going to be okay?"

Looking up at the other Princess Amara, I noted how concern flickered in her eyes for a brief moment before they narrowed back at me. "Why do you care? You did this to her!"

"What? No, I didn't! I would never hurt her." My eyes narrowed right back at hers as agitation built in my core. "I came to talk to her, and like I said, those things attacked again. Not that I have to explain myself to *you.*"

"Then why the hell do you not seem fazed in the slightest by seeing the both of us. Admit it, *you're* the one who did this to her!" She lunged toward me with her arms raised, fire blazing in her eyes, but before she could lay a finger on me, the Lord Regent caught her and pulled her back.

"You're psychotic, you know that? I thought I was crazy for how I felt, but this makes much more sense." My fingers gestured between the two identical women. "I am not fazed because I already figured it out earlier. When I bumped into you... or *her*, or whoever the hell I ran into earlier today, she, or you, or *they* seemed upset." *Gods,* it was all so confusing. "I wanted to talk to you. I mean *her*—" I closed my eyes, lips pressing into a line from exasperation. "Anyways, I went to your bed chambers, where I found Lord Chaz of Caelia rummaging around, clearly looking for something. When I confronted him, I noticed that he had dropped something, so I quickly grabbed it and hid it before he could retrieve it. Once he was gone, I saw that it was a journal, and I was planning on returning it to you when…." My voice trailed off as my hand disappeared into my jacket pocket. "This photo fell out of it."

Pulling the journal out of my pocket, I held it up for her to see before tugging the photo from its spine. The image was of the King and Queen standing side by side, each with an identical blonde baby tucked in their arms. "It wouldn't take a genius to put two and two together. Once you open your mouths, you two are so different you might as well be night and day."

She just stood there, dumbfounded, her eyes wide and mouth hanging open. Her eyes flitted from the contents in my hands to me and back.

"Here," I grumbled as I handed them over to her.

"Oh. Thank you... I guess." She mumbled as she took them, examining the photo quickly before handing them off to the Regent.

"Well, then, *I guess* you're welcome. Now, can we focus on the real issues at hand here? What really happened? How can we help her?"

"I'm still not convinced of your innocence," she replied dryly, crossing her arms and raising a brow.

I scoffed. "How do I know *you're* not the one who did this? Where have you been while she's been here?"

She flinched at the accusation, and I suspected it took a lot of effort to not lunge at me again. "That is none of your business, and she's my sister; I would never!"

"Yeah, well, she's my... *my friend*." My voice lowered at the last part as my gaze landed on the woman in question, still lying helplessly on the ground. "I… I don't even know her name, assuming that you are the real Princess Amara, of course."

"Her Highness is not to blame… and I do not believe Prince Alexander is to blame either." Lord Regent chimed in, looking at me and then at Princess Amara beside him. I was thankful that *he* at least seemed to have his head together. "He is correct; we need to bring Avery to a healer and out of the halls where anyone could see us."

Avery.

I looked down at her, savoring the name in my mind.

I opened my mouth to say it aloud, but a crash sliced through the silence before I could even utter the first syllable. I moved before I knew what was happening, practically diving over Avery's body to protect her from the shards of glass that rained down from the shattering windows. We all ducked low to the ground, and I looked back at Princess Amara as she stared at me in complete shock. As soon as our eyes met, hers narrowed, her brows scrunching together as she watched me.

I didn't even have time to say anything before another window shattered. A deafening shriek sounded as shadow demons surged in and flooded the halls. Cries of terror echoed around us, letting us know they had likely infiltrated the entire castle. Everything was hazy as darkness seeped through the broken windows like smoke.

"We have to go! Now!" Amara stood, helping the Regent to his feet. I moved swiftly, pulling myself and Avery off the floor and cradling her in my arms. I needed to get her somewhere safe. Fast.

"Lead the way," I gritted out.

Amara's eyes closed, and the rise and fall of her chest slowed with each breath. I watched her carefully, unsure what the hell she was doing.

"Stay close!" she called out as she suddenly took off down the corridor.

A bright, golden light shot out, radiating off her entire body. I jerked back, turning my head to the side and squinting my eyes as I waited for them to adjust. When they did, I couldn't believe what I saw as that same light expanded out and completely surrounded all four of us.

I stared after her in awe as she kept moving down the corridor, my feet planted in place until all the noise in the space brought me back to reality.

It only took me another moment before I realized I needed to follow.

CHAPTER THREE

Amara

I didn't look back as I ran. Footsteps thumping behind me were the only indicator that they were still with me.

The castle was swarming with shadow demons and screams echoed in the corridors as we ran. We needed to get somewhere safe.

The infirmary.

I took a sharp left and raced down the stairs. I quickly glanced over my shoulder to confirm they were still with me inside my barrier.

My barrier felt stronger than before. I could feel its warmth swirling inside of me, as if it were part of my soul. Demon after demon made contact with the barrier, and I watched as my light ripped each of them apart from the inside out, rendering them nothing more than ash and dust.

"Holy shit!" Xander exclaimed, "How did you do that?"

"I don't know. Why don't you touch the barrier and see for yourself?" I cast a mischievous look over my shoulder as we moved closer to the infirmary. He rolled his eyes, his arms flexing as he tightened his grip on Avery.

I opened the door as they ran in, slamming it shut and locking it behind us once we were safely inside. A split second later, the door started rattling as demons clawed at its surface and screeched from the other side.

A warm, tingling sensation ran along my skin as my body continued to radiate the golden glow. I shut my eyes and imagined what I wanted to happen. *I need the light to keep us safe. I need the light to grow and rid the entire palace of these demons.*

As the light flew out of me, it took my breath with it, and I staggered back for a moment. The terrifying sounds stopped just as I regained my composure. I stared in amazement, then looked at Lawrence and Xander, who were both as astonished as I was. I reached for the door, but Lawrence threw his arm out, stopping me before I could open it.

"Your Highness, wait! It could be a trap! Please, allow me," he said as he gently pushed me behind him, as if it would do anything if those things were still out there. Lawrence carefully opened the door just enough for him to peek through. "They're gone," he breathed.

I let out a sigh of relief before turning to look back at Xander and watched as he slowly lowered Avery down onto one of the beds.

"Is—Is it safe?" A soft voice trembled from inside a large medicine cabinet.

"Yes," I answered as I stepped toward it.

A small woman stepped out of it and instantly froze as she looked at us.

"Your Highness." She curtsied low. "I—I wasn't aware that it was you in here. I am sorry." She looked from me to Avery on the bed and then back, her eyes widening.

Before I could even think of what I should say, Lawrence stepped forward.

"Miss Wagner, as you can see, we do require your assistance."

"Oh! Of course." She didn't hesitate as she moved to examine Avery.

"And it would be best if this were to stay between those of us in this room," Lawrence added, to which Miss Wagner nodded in agreement.

Xander remained by Avery's side as Miss Wagner performed her examination. Glancing over at Lawrence and catching his gaze, I jerked my head toward the other side of the room. I then waited for him to follow me there, keeping my eye on Xander and Avery the entire time.

"What do you think happened to her?" I whispered.

"I am not sure. As I mentioned, I believe there is a mole within the castle. Whoever it is must be working with this Shadow Lord and may even be using the same kind of magical gifts you possess."

"Magical gifts?" Xander's voice came from behind me, and I turned to see him standing only inches away from us.

I rolled my eyes. "I thought you were with Avery."

"And I thought it was suspicious that you decided to go and whisper secrets in a corner. I guess I was right to think so."

"You know, it is rude to eavesdrop on private conversations," I countered.

"It's *rude* to have private conversations while others are in the room, especially when it concerns them."

"How does any of this concern *you*?" I almost laughed at how ridiculous that statement was.

"How does it not? I was the one who came to help her. I was the one who caught her when she fell—"

"Assuming you aren't the reason why she is in this state," I interjected.

"I would *never* hurt her," he clipped, clearly agitated. "But I think I know who would... and who this mole you speak of may be."

"You are not a part of this," I snapped, turning back to face him fully. He had no idea what these things were or what they could do. I barely knew myself, so how could he possibly know anything?

"I was the one who was there for her when they attacked us multiple times. Where were you? Off gallivanting with gods know who?"

My arms crossed over my chest in defiance. "Not that it's any of your business, but I was trying to find the Solunian prophecy so I wouldn't be stuck marrying *you*." My grin was smug as I stared him down. But a moment later, my face fell, the realization that I'd said too much striking me. Hard.

My mouth slowly dropped open as a jolt of panic ran through me, my arms dropping to my sides as my gaze restlessly shifted to Lawrence and back.

He scoffed a laugh. "Oh, my mistake. You were off playing make-believe while you left Avery here to fend for herself. Where did she even come from? Where has she been all these years?" His eyes narrowed on me. "Just because I figured out that there were two of you doesn't mean I don't have more questions and need more answers."

"The only thing you *need* to do is *leave*," I shouted, arms raised as if I were about to physically push him out the door.

"Will you both stop acting like spoiled children and think of Avery!" Lawrence's voice raised, and I could not remember ever hearing him sound so angry. "Amara, I believe Prince Xander does indeed care for your sister, and we could use the help." Taking a moment to compose himself, his chest raised as he inhaled a deep breath and adjusted his tie. He turned to Xander before continuing. "You said you had an idea of who this mole may be. Please elaborate."

"Like I said, I had gone looking for you in your bed chambers earlier, and I found Lord Chaz snooping around. It was dark; he hadn't even turned a single light on. I thought it was you at first, and when I called out your name, I must have startled him. He seemed nervous and fidgety and could not have gotten out of there fast enough after that. Why else would he have been in there?" Xander shrugged a shoulder, and although he had a solid point, I knew it was possible that Chaz could have been in there trying to dig up dirt on me to further strengthen his claim to the throne.

"We need more evidence. I will admit it is possible, but Chaz wants to be king. Why would he bring demons to destroy what he wants so strongly?" I sighed. How were we supposed to figure out who this mole was with so many people in the castle?

Lawrence cleared his throat, "Why don't we think of a few possible suspects and investigate discreetly? We'll keep an eye on our top suspects and report back with our findings. Xander, you keep an eye on the Duke of Caelia." Xander surprised me as he chose not to fight or argue and didn't complain about how this was not his kingdom or problem.

He just nodded in agreement as his eyes landed back on Avery.

"Amara, do you have any idea who it could be?" Lawrence asked, drawing my attention back to him and off of Xander and Avery.

"I do not. I have not been here for a while; maybe it would be best if you were to assign me someone you suspect, Lawrence." Trying my best not to show my disappointment, I faked a smile. This was my kingdom, and it was in danger. Someone in the kingdom was working with the enemy, and I hadn't a clue who that might have been.

"Right, of course." Lawrence looked at me with pity in his eyes that I did not need or deserve. This was my fault, and I had to be the one to fix it, so I would do exactly that.

I was surprised when Xander was the one to speak.

"Why don't you put the castle on lockdown? No one gets in or out. Whoever it was must still be here, somewhere within these walls. I'll investigate Lord Chaz. Lawrence, you keep an eye on things and make sure that the lockdown is running smoothly, including keeping tabs on any visitors." As Lawrence nodded, Xander shifted his attention back to me. "Amara, look into anyone who has permanent residence in the castle. We can meet back tomorrow with anything we find."

I blinked at him in surprise. "That—That's actually an excellent plan."

"Right. I will go and track Chaz down. We all know what we need to do now." Xander nodded curtly before moving back to Avery's side.

I was distracted by the concern that etched itself into his expression, and I didn't miss the way he gently grasped her hand in his. He took a deep breath as he watched her, then stood abruptly and exited the room without so much as another word or glance in my direction.

Lawrence looked at me with a sympathetic, almost pitying expression before he, too, left, leaving me alone with only my thoughts.

This entire situation was my fault. I should have been here. Everyone was in danger and suffering as a result of my actions.

Making my way back through the corridors, I tried to keep an eye out for anything suspicious, but what did I know about what really went on in the castle? I probably could not name a single guest or staff member. I did not even know who my new attendant was supposed to be, and oh gods… *Wes.* He had risked everything to get me out of the Shadowlands, and for what?

I knew I should try to think positively, but my head and my heart were filled with so many warring thoughts and emotions that it seemed nearly impossible.

I needed a distraction. Fast.

My silent plea was heard and granted as I rounded the corner and nearly collided with Erik, his strong arms helping to steady me as I staggered back.

"Amara," he breathed as I tried to hold myself together, forever refusing to let anyone see me break. "Is everything okay? I just heard the castle is going into lockdown."

Lawrence works fast.

"Yes," I answered as I double-checked that no one else was nearby. As soon as I was confident that we were alone, I shoved Erik up against the wall. "I need this," I whispered, pressing my body against his, our lips only a breath apart.

His gaze immediately dropped to my mouth before flicking back to meet mine.

"I thought you wanted this to be over?"

"Maybe I just need one last distraction," I confessed, desperation lacing my tone.

He looked over my shoulder before spinning me until my back was against the wall, his hands still gripped around my waist. "Allow me to be your distraction then, my queen," Erik drawled before dropping to his knees before me.

His hands slowly trailed up my thighs, and my eyes followed him as he smirked up at me. Keeping his eyes on me, his lips grazed my inner thigh, and I instantly felt my cheeks warm.

Dropping my head back against the wall and closing my eyes, I tried my best to live in the moment, but as soon as my eyes shut, I only saw one face.

Wesley's.

"Wait!" I blurted suddenly, too loudly, as my eyes flashed open.

Erik jerked back instantly, and I immediately felt his absence as the cool air rushed in and replaced the warmth that his lips and hands had provided.

"What's wrong?" He asked as I grabbed his hand and ushered him back to his feet.

"It is just… I cannot. Not anymore. I am sorry." I turned to leave, but he stopped me with a hand on my shoulder.

"You do not need to apologize. This was always supposed to be fun and meaningless, but I think we both know we let it go on much longer than it should have." His lips lifted before stepping back to let me pass.

"You are right, and I am sorry if I led you on in any way. It is just… *complicated.*"

"Is there someone else?" he asked, but his tone was not jealous. It was as if he could sense I needed to talk about it.

"There is," I forced a tight smile. "But it will never work. He deserves more than I could ever give him. He deserves to be happy."

Erik placed a hand on my cheek, his smile warm. "*You* deserve to be happy too."

As Erik walked away, I stood there motionless, transfixed.

Why is everyone pitying me today?

Turning around and returning the way I came, I was relieved to find myself completely alone.

We had a plan, and we needed to figure out who the traitor inside the castle was. Once they were dealt with, I could focus on the demons.

I could focus on saving Wesley.

CHAPTER FOUR

Avery

This was it. I was returning to college to figure out what I wanted to do with the rest of my life. This should have been easy, right? Most people knew this well before the age of twenty, but here I was. I hoped people wouldn't judge me for being old. It wasn't like I was *that* much older than everyone else there.

Why did I always have to get into my head about these kinds of things? From my experience, people probably wouldn't even notice me, and if they did, they probably wouldn't care. Returning to college was supposed to be fun and exciting, so why did I have a knot in my stomach the size of a truck?

Okay, relax, Avery! This will be fun! It's just orientation.

Exhaling a long breath, I tried to steady my mind. My meeting with the Chancellor had actually gone great. Not only did I get my schedule and everything sorted out, but I received news that my tuition had been paid in full by some anonymous source. They even offered me free housing on campus, which I told them I had to consider. By the sounds of it, the on-campus apartment sounded larger than my current apartment. And sure, I would have a roommate with whom I would have to share the living space, but free rent? Who could pass up an opportunity like that?

Finally making it to campus, I stood in the courtyard and stared up at the old building. It reminded me of one of those magical schools in books where the students get to learn all sorts of charms and potions. I was fairly certain this was not that kind of school, though I would have to admit that it would be fantastic if it was. Who cares about figuring my life out when I could just magic up whatever I wanted?

Students and faculty buzzed around the campus, talking and laughing. Everyone seemed to enjoy themselves, and I hoped I would soon be doing the same. The sun shone brightly, and there wasn't a cloud in the sky. Everything and everyone seemed picture-perfect.

Everything but *me*.

Continuing down the main path that led to the giant building, I tried to keep my head down and avoid any attention. To my surprise, everyone I passed smiled or nodded a greeting in my direction. Sure, that probably sounded nice in theory, but I found it unsettling, almost creepy.

I wanted to smile back, wave, and maybe even introduce myself, but whenever I looked back at someone, I either froze or couldn't find the words. The one time I managed to get something out, I ended up mixing 'hi' and 'hello' together and greeted them with a 'hi-o.'

Smooth, Avery.

On the opposite side of the courtyard, I noticed tents with people giving out pamphlets and flyers about various school groups and activities. Making my way over there, I figured I was bound to find something that interested me. A book club or movie marathon club could be cool... if they even had those.

I held my head up high as I went over the customary greetings people used in my head on my way to registration. *Hi. Hello. Nice to meet you.* Totally normal. Though I didn't manage to say any of these things, I did smile at a couple different people as I made my way down the path. It was pathetic, sure, but it was still progress.

The registration booth's bright red sign was close, only a few steps away. I quickened my pace, and just as I was about to reach the table, a hand holding a flyer shot out in front of me.

Blinking in surprise, I slowly took the flyer and turned to the person who handed it to me. It was a friendly-looking woman who looked about my age with long, wavy dark hair, green eyes, and a giant smile.

"We are always looking for new members for our book club." Her smile somehow managed to grow even wider.

"Thank you," I mumbled as I looked back down at the flyer. It was for a book club that took place bi-weekly, and the first book on the list just so happened to be for my favourite series about a school for the supernatural.

"I love this series! Though I must admit, it is more of an obsession than anything else." I hadn't even meant to say that, but the woman spoke before I could feel embarrassed about my admission.

"Right? I binged them way too fast the first time I read them," she laughed, and I couldn't help but join in. "I'm Meresay. But you can just call me Mer." She extended her hand, and I shook it quickly before letting go.

"Avery." I gave a curt nod before glancing back at the flyer.

"Well, Avery, I hope to see you at the first club meeting in the library in a few days so we can discuss all things books!"

"Yes, I'd like that." I didn't even have to fake a smile as I looked back at her. Something about her seemed so familiar, but I couldn't quite place it. "I have to go register, but... thank you."

I took off before she could answer, but the smile didn't leave my face.

If only making friends was always that easy.

The sun was setting, which meant that the deadline to decide whether I wanted to live on campus was soon. And by soon, that meant the duration of time that it took me to find the Chancellor's office again. It seemed too good of an opportunity to pass up, so admittedly I was leaning toward a yes.

It wasn't like I would have to attend all the campus parties and events if I did live on campus, even if I did, it would probably help with my confidence issues. Plus, living on campus meant living close to a 24-hour library, which was another obvious point in the "yes" column. Who *wouldn't* want to live close to a library?

"Did you need help finding something?" A male voice cut through my inner babbling, and I looked up a split second before I nearly walked straight into him.

"I... uh—" I stammered, trying and failing to answer. I didn't think it would have been that difficult to answer him until my gaze met the ocean-blue hue of his.

"You?" He said as a smirk pulled at the corner of his lips, which were somehow even more distracting than his eyes.

"Yes." I cleared my throat but was at another loss once his gaze met mine again.

He huffed a laugh while he tried to cover his smile with his hand. "It's just... I've seen you pass by this same hallway three times now and figured you might be lost." He quirked a brow, no longer trying to hide his grin.

"Yes, well—wait. Have you just been watching me the entire time?" My eyes narrowed as I took a slow step backward and further away from him.

"Maybe," He laughed. "But not on purpose. I was in that room, and it was hard to miss the same honey-gold hair passing by that many times. Who knows how many times you walked by before I noticed and how many more you would have if I wasn't so kind as to come out and offer my assistance?"

"I suppose I should be thanking my hair for being so noticeable then." I shocked myself with that. Was I just... *flirting*? It was so unlike me. I would never in a million years say something like that, so why had I just then? "I'm trying to find the Chancellor's office," I quickly added before he could comment.

"I could take you there if you'd like. Wouldn't want you to get even more lost than you are now."

Astonished, I watched as he walked down the corridor. No "Right this way" or anything. He just started walking. I shook my head in disbelief before catching up to him.

Who is this guy? And why am I following him?

I was even more taken aback by the fact that he didn't say a single thing as he led the way. What if he wasn't even really taking me to the Chancellor? What if he was taking me back to his place? Or leading me to some random room to get me alone? What if he was just some random guy who didn't even go to school here?

"Well, here we are." His thumb nonchalantly pointed to a door, *"Chancellor Le" scrawled across it.*

I turned back to thank him, but he had already started back down the hallway.

"Thank you," I called out to him, and he waved a hand dismissively without even looking back.

Before I could raise my hand to knock on the door, it swung open. I probably shouldn't have been that surprised since I just yelled right in front of it.

"Ah, Miss Bate. You made it. Welcome." He gestured me in as he continued to hold the door open.

"Thank you, Sir," I said as I stepped into his office.

"Please, have a seat."

I took the chair opposite his desk and waited for him to sit.

"How did you find orientation today?" He asked as he took his seat.

"It was great, thank you."

"I'm glad to hear it. It goes until the end of the week, you know. Plenty of fun activities for anyone who wants to participate."

"That sounds fun." I tried my best to paint a somewhat believable-looking smile on my face.

"Yes, well, you young kids always seem to have the best time. Anyways, let us not beat around the bush. Have you made a decision regarding your living arrangements? I had your room assignment and keys prepared, just in case." He adjusted his thin-rimmed glasses before looking through a pile of papers scattered atop his desk.

"Yes, I would love to accept the on-campus housing offer. Thank you so much again for this opportunity." My smile was genuine as he looked up at me in surprise, then adjusted his tie before he rose from his seat and extended his hand.

"Of course, we would be glad to have you," he returned as he firmly shook my hand. Chancellor Le slid one of the papers he had been looking at moments ago toward me with a pen and keycard atop it. "I just need your signature; then you are free to move in at your earliest convenience."

"Great," I smiled, grabbing the pen and signing on the required lines, then pocketed the keycard before sliding the paper and pen back to him.

"You will be staying in Skylar Hall, room 402A." He said as he read the room number off the paper in front of him.

I stood there for a few moments as he silently returned to his pile of paperwork, wondering if that was all, before finally repeating my thanks and leaving.

On my way back through the halls, I tried to remember anything that could be some kind of landmark to remember how to get back should I ever need to. Much like the school's exterior, the hallways reminded me of the dimly-lit corridors one would find in a castle, with doors every few feet that all looked identical. How was I ever going to find my way around? I was bad enough with directions as it was.

My first class didn't start until noon the next day, so I figured I might as well go back to my apartment, pack up, and move everything I needed to my new place in the morning. Luckily, since my apartment had been fully furnished upon move-in, I didn't have too many things to move out with me. And thankfully, I didn't need to worry about procuring furniture for the new place either.

But even knowing how painless of a process moving would be, my nerves were still flaring at the thought of how quickly things were changing.

This was going to be a good thing. Right?

CHAPTER FIVE

Xander

Duke Ashburn of Caelia always spent much of his time in the castle gardens, so I figured I should start there. As soon as I made my way out there, I was bombarded with thoughts of Princess Ama—*Avery*. Everywhere I looked, I saw flashes of her—watching her sit for hours with that attendant Bartholomew, petting Stark, dancing in the rain under the faint moonlight.

I shook my head to clear it, trying to get my mind back on the task at hand. There was no sign of Chaz, but it was a large garden, so I did another sweep around just to be safe.

But as I approached the hedge maze, I remembered how just beyond it was the pond where Avery and I danced together. It was so apparent that she was different, not that I knew much about the real Princess Amara, but something just felt different with Avery. Things were easier with her.

Though I didn't know what happened to Avery, I was certain we would be able to wake her up and find whoever was responsible for this. It had to be the Duke. There was always something off about him. Of course, I always blamed it on their whole family being unlikeable, but clearly, I had been wrong about that.

He wasn't there, but I found that I didn't have it in me to leave just then. Stepping closer to the pond, I thought about my wish that night and how Avery put that whole night together for all of us. She didn't have to, but she did. I barely even knew her, but I wanted to know more; I wanted to know *everything*.

I opened up to her about my father. I told her things that I hadn't told anyone else. Of course, Hazel knew most of it. She witnessed firsthand how cruel our father was. Not even Erik or Victoria knew everything, but somehow, I felt like I could trust her with it. I had only told her where it all started, but I was beginning to feel like I could tell her even more about how much of a monster he truly was.

Closing my eyes, I let out a long shaky breath. We had this truce that had admittedly become so much more to me. Once I finally opened my eyes, I stared at the spot where we danced and hoped it would not be our last.

Walking back toward the main gardens, more people had begun to congregate around them. With the lockdown keeping everyone inside the kingdom, it made sense that the gardens would have been a popular choice.

Even though I was fairly certain that Duke Ashburn was the traitor, I couldn't help but wonder if any of the other people I saw could also be behind this. I didn't want to rule anyone out, just in case.

The Duke wasn't in the gardens. Regardless of where he might have been instead, I was glad to be able to cross this off my list for the time being.

When I entered the castle, Victoria immediately spotted me, appearing to stop mid-sentence in her conversation with Hazel to wave me over.

"We're so glad you're okay!" Hazel said as she and Victoria pulled me into a weird group hug.

The guilt sank in at that moment. Considering what had just occurred, why didn't I think to check on my friends and sister before searching for the Duke? The realization caused me to tighten my grip a little more as I held them.

Seconds before letting them go, I mumbled, "I'm so glad you're both safe."

"What the hell happened, and why are we now in lockdown?" Vic asked, not realizing that I actually knew the answer, at least to some extent.

Debating whether or not to tell them everything, I concluded that I should wait. Until we managed to find out who was responsible for this, the fewer people that knew, the better.

"The castle was under attack by more of those shadow demons," I whispered, looking over my shoulder nervously.

Victoria's eyes grew wide. Then I remembered she hadn't seen any of them, and I wondered if she'd even heard of them. Hazel was with us when we ran into them in the alley, so she could have told her, but her expression suggested otherwise.

Hazel and I shared a look, causing Vic to snap.

"What the fuck aren't you two telling me?"

"There's a lot we need to tell you. We don't even know how or why it's happening, but you should know so we can be prepared." The comforting touch of Hazel's hand on her shoulder made her face soften slightly.

"Okay. Then explain."

"Hazel, you fill her in. I will meet up with you in a bit. There is something I want to check on." When Hazel gave me her trademark death stare for abandoning her, I just shrugged my shoulders, already backing away as a smirk pulled over my lips. Before she could utter a word, I took a quick left and disappeared down a corridor.

Aside from Chaz Ashburn, there was one other person I needed to search for: Erik. I wanted to find him to be sure he was safe, not because I suspected he was guilty.

CHAPTER SIX

Amara

I needed to come up with a list of suspects, but so far, I had none. As much as I would hate to have to tell Xander he was right, the one person I could think of was Chaz. But why would he attack a kingdom he wanted to rule? It did not make sense to me. I had been gone for a while, there had to be something I was missing, and I was determined to find it.

"Amara!" Someone shouted from down the corridor. *Wesley?* My mind automatically assumed as so few addressed me without a title. However, as I turned around, I came face to face with a man I did not recognize.

"I was waiting in the garden for you when those things attacked. I was so worried I had failed you. I'm so glad you're alright." He flashed a relieved smile as I studied him.

Am I supposed to know him? Why was he waiting for me in the garden?

He must have read the confusion on my face as he spoke again.

"I'm sorry, were we not to meet in the garden today? I brought snacks," he said as he held up a picnic basket. "You are okay, aren't you? I knew I should have walked with you to the garden. It is my job, and something could have happened. We were under attack, and I wasn't there. I should be fired or—"

"It is fine." For the sake of silence, I cut him off.

Realization hit me. *He must have been Wesley's replacement while we were gone.* Clearly, he and Avery had been friendly. *I should investigate him more. But perhaps, for now, I should play along. I don't want to raise suspicion.*

"I was on my way there when the attack occurred. I am glad you are okay." I gave him a confident, reassuring smile.

"I also brought a few books I think you would like; they are some of my favourites." We started down the corridor toward the gardens, and as my stomach growled, he laughed as he held up the basket again. "I guess it's a good thing I brought these."

I had to admit I was curious about what kind of so-called snacks were in that basket. It had been a while since I had anything good.

We proceeded to the gardens, where he began to ramble on and on about his poetry. I nodded along as if I understood. Once we arrived, he brought us to a tree where a blanket was already laid beneath, and we sat down. I blinked as I watched in surprise.

Did they do this often?

Glancing around, the few people that spotted us paid no attention, as if this was a regular occurrence.

Slowly, I sat down on the blanket. He pulled out cheeses, bread, and fruit and started laying them into the space between us on the blanket. Then he pulled out a notebook and started writing, picking away at food without even looking up from the papers.

Looking around once more for any clue as to what Avery—as me—would do in a situation like this, I found myself at a complete loss.

Once I turned back toward him, I realized he had been watching me. "Did you forget to bring a book or something to read today? Here, you can start one of the ones I brought for you if you'd like," he said as he pulled three books out from the bottom of the basket.

"Thank you," I said while slowly reaching over to take one of the books from his hands.

His smile beamed at me briefly before he returned to whatever he was writing.

I opened the book and pretended to read while scanning the garden. Guards and servants wandered about as we sat silently, smiling and bowing to me as they passed.

Ignoring them, my eyes skimmed the pages of the book I was holding, turning pages as if I wasn't completely distracted by my own thoughts. How was I to determine who was responsible for any of this? I was not sure, but I needed to figure it out quickly in addition to figuring out how to awaken Avery and rescue Wesley.

Placing the book down, I reached for the food that was brought. I could not do any of this if I did not eat anything first. I needed to leave this garden and speak with Lawrence. Perhaps we could devise another plan.

The moment I rose to my feet, his gaze locked on mine.

I cleared my throat before I spoke. "There is a meeting I have to attend with the Lord Regent. Your presence is not required, so please take this time for yourself."

Instead of waiting for him to reply, I quickly turned around and started walking back toward the castle, heading straight for Lawrence's office. I was almost certain that was where I would find him.

I quickly knocked before opening the door. Lawrence was exactly where I expected him to be. Sitting at his desk, going through piles of paperwork. I closed the door before moving to take the seat in front of his desk.

His eyes shifted toward me. "No luck, I suppose?"

"Afraid not. There must be an easier way to do this. There are nearly one hundred people within the castle right now.

What am I to do? Ask everyone if they have done or seen anything suspicious lately?"

"That is not the worst idea," he answered. My eyes narrowed as I tried to figure out if this was part of his odd sense of humor before he continued. "It is not as though we were the only ones to have seen what happened or been under attack. It would not be that hard to believe we would interview some people about it."

"Interview or interrogate?" I laughed while he shook his head as he examined the papers on his desk.

"Here is a list of potential suspects you can start with. It is rather lengthy, and as you have stated, it could be anyone." He passed me a stack of papers, and I huffed a breath. It had been more extensive than I had hoped, but at least it was a start.

"There must be something else we can do… some way for my power to grow stronger so I can protect everyone. The dreams I had about this Shadow Lord had to be more than dreams, and they mentioned something about a grimoire, which did not sound good for us." I raked my hands through my hair and closed my eyes, trying and failing to calm myself and remember anything else from my dreams that could help.

When I looked back at Lawrence, he was at the bookshelf behind his desk. He took several off the shelf before handing them to me.

"I had always planned to give you these, but I wanted to hang on to them for as long as possible."

Staring down at the outdated leather-bound books, I opened a page for some clarity as to what they might have been. The pages were old and all in different handwriting. Confused, I met his eyes again.

The sadness and despair that flashed behind his eyes were palpable. "They were Liliana's."

A shaky breath escaped my lips as he turned away.

Lawrence rarely spoke of his sister. The only things I knew of Liliana were that she was his older sister and that she had died well before I was ever born.

With his back still to me, he spoke again. "She was a Celestial."

CHAPTER SEVEN

Avery

My new roommate was not present the entire time I hauled my stuff into my new apartment. Based on the bookcases full of some of my favourite books on display in the living room, I was confident this could be the start of a great friendship. Of course, that was if I could manage to not make a complete fool out of myself once I did finally meet them.

"Only you," a soft voice whispered behind me, making me jump in alarm and drop the small cardboard box I had in my hands. When I turned to see the face behind the voice, there was no one there. Shaking my head in disbelief as I searched the room, I confirmed that I was still very much alone.

"I must be hearing things," I told myself as I bent over to grab the box again and bring it into my bedroom.

The room was a decent size, especially when considering I didn't technically have a bedroom in my old bachelor floor plan.

Placing the box down next to the bed, I took in the room around me. It was painted a lovely lavender. My favourite. It would match my bedding so perfectly. What were the chances?

Hanging up all my clothes and unpacking the few boxes I had, I was done unpacking with plenty of time to spare before my first class. *I could probably fit an episode of something in before class.*

As I made my way back into the common area of our apartment, the main door opened.

When the girl from the book club booth entered, her green eyes locked on mine. Her smile beaming brightly as she stepped toward me.

"No way! You're my new roommate?" Despite my best efforts to dodge it, Meresay wrapped her arms around me as I tried to get her off me without making the situation unpleasant. No offense to her, but I was never one for bear hugs, especially with people I barely knew.

"Only you."

"Excuse me?" My brow quirked as I questioned her.

"Oops, sorry. Are you not big on hugs?"

"No, it's just… sorry, never mind." I turned away from her, my head slightly shaking in confusion as I aimed to retreat into my room.

"This is wonderful!" she called after me. "I hoped to see you again soon. I just assumed it would be at book club. This is even better!" The excitement she exuded compelled me to face her once more.

"Yeah, I was actually hoping to join the book club." Painting on my brightest smile, I tried to seem as enthusiastic as possible.

"Great, feel free to borrow any of my books anytime!" She gestured toward the many bookcases lining the walls of the shared living space.

Quickly scanning the shelves, I already noted several books I knew I would be taking her up on that offer with.

"Thank you." This time, my grin was sincere, and I didn't dare look away from the bookcases for a few moments.

Her green eyes locked on mine once I averted my gaze from the books. My stomach clenched as I realized she'd been watching me. Something about her seemed so familiar, yet I couldn't place it. Perhaps we had run into each other before at a bookstore or library. Or maybe she just had one of those faces. The more I thought about it, the more I figured it was probably the latter.

"I should finish unpacking before class," I said, finally breaking the silence as she watched me. Once I was alone again, a slightly guilty feeling settled in my stomach. I didn't know why I lied.

As I locked myself in my room, my reflection in the mirror hanging on the back of the door drew my attention. It didn't feel like I was actually gazing back at myself. Even though I had no idea how to style my hair this way, my hair was in a stunning updo I had never done before.

My eyes continued down, and I was even more surprised by my blue and gold patterned dress. The elegant embroidery of gold stitched along the blue bodice was almost regal. A flash of gold caught my attention. A tiara sat atop my head. I reached up to touch it, blinking in disbelief. A moment later, it vanished.

As I rubbed my eyes, I noticed that my dress had been replaced by leggings and a t-shirt. My hair down, loose curls falling past my shoulders. My stomach squeezed; I knew something was off. Surely, I reasoned, this was all in my head.

A soft knock on my door startled me out of my stupor. Slowly opening the door a crack, I peered out to find Meresay standing before me.

"You forgot this," she said as she handed me my phone through the opening.

"Thanks," I replied with a tight smile. I glanced down at my phone and read the time on the home screen. "Shit, I'm going to be late."

Meresay stood by the side of the hallway as I ran out of the apartment, scooping up the luggage that I had left in the common area before racing out.

Where did the time go? When I realized that my first class was starting in ten minutes, I knew I had to sprint to get there in time. God, I really wasn't a fan of running.

On the bright side, this wasn't high school, so it wasn't like I had to beat some bell. But what would be the point of coming here if I didn't actually attend the classes?

In front of the door, I almost collapsed, my hands on my knees as I struggled for air. This was pathetic. Breathing in slowly, I straightened my back and combed my fingers through my hair before entering the classroom with smooth steps.

The lecture hall was huge, more like an auditorium than anything else, with the professor seated at a large desk full of papers with a whiteboard behind it. So many empty seats were left for the picking, so I grabbed one of the closest spots to where I entered in the second to last row.

Glancing at the clock, I noted that it was now three minutes past when the class was set to start. Anxiously tapping my pen on the desk, I waited for the professor to do something. A throat cleared behind me, and I peeked over my shoulder to see that guy from the other day watching me.

"Are you going to be doing that all class? If so, I might as well move now." The side of his mouth twitched upward as I glared at him.

"Well, if it bothers you that much," I said as I faced the front again and continued tapping it, only harder and louder this time.

He breathed a laugh behind me, and I couldn't help my smile as he did. The next second, he climbed over the back of the seat next to me and plopped down.

"I thought you said you were going to move if I didn't stop?" I shot him a sideways glance, keeping my face straight toward the front of the class.

"Oh, but I did. See, I was sitting back there." He gestured behind us with his thumb, "And now I'm sitting here." He stretched his arms wide before placing an elbow on my desk, practically pushing my notebook off.

"Seriously?"

"You could always move." He smirked at me again.

"I was here first," I bit out through clenched teeth.

His only response was a slight chuckle before finally removing his arm from my tiny desk. He didn't get up and move, but neither did I.

Then the professor finally stood up and wrote their name on the board.

When class was finally over, I swiftly gathered my stuff and left. We hadn't spoken another word to one another for the rest of class, though I kept feeling as if he was watching me out of the corner of his eye. I refused to let him catch me looking back.

"Hey, wait up!" he called as he ran after me.

Continuing down the hallway, I pretended I couldn't hear him.

"I know you can hear me!" he shouted. Clearly, I was not a good actress.

Just as he had done to me the day before, I waved him off without a second thought.

The sounds of his footsteps echoed as he caught up to me. I quickened my steps, but it was no use. He was next to me within seconds, his steps slowing to match mine.

"I like you." I caught a glimpse of his mouth quirking to one side out of the corner of my eye.

I rolled my eyes. "You don't even know me."

"But I'd like to." Stopping mid-step, I stared at him with a raised brow. "What's your name?" He asked with a flirtatious smile.

Turning down a hallway, I tried my best not to roll my eyes yet again. He made a speedy recovery and was back by my side once again.

"Fine," he chuckled. "I'll go first. I'm Alec." Still refusing to break my silence, he spoke again. "And you are?"

"Avery. My name is Avery," I conceded.

"Okay, Avery. Well, I hope to see you around." And just like that, he spun around and walked away.

What had been the point of all that? Just to get my name? It didn't make any sense.

As I made a second turn down a hallway, it was as if everything went dark. There were no other people around, and as I approached one of the windows, it appeared as though the sun had completely vanished. The moon had not appeared in its absence, and there weren't even stars to light the sky. It was just black nothingness.

As my eyes finally adjusted to the darkness, I noticed how the air turned thick and foggy, almost as if a cloud of smoke was swirling around me. My brows furrowed as I looked this way and that, my ears suddenly picking up on the sounds of hushed voices. I tried my best to make out the words, but the way the sounds started to move in and out and dance around me was almost disorienting, causing my eyes to slam shut as a chill ran down my spine.

After taking several slow steps back, I broke into a full-on sprint, the corridor seeming to grow longer and longer as I raced down it. I chanced a look back over my shoulder as I ran, and it was as if it went on forever in both directions.

Faint light glowed around me. I couldn't tell where it was coming from, but it made it slightly easier to see a short distance in front of me. Classroom doors appeared, and I tried opening a few. Every door I opened just led to a blackhole of darkness. I yanked another door open, and this time, I came face to face with a figure, shrouded in shadows, its face concealed by a dark cloak.

I screamed, taking several slow steps back, too afraid to do anything else as my gaze locked on them. I couldn't see their eyes, but I could tell from the way the energy shifted in the room that their attention was solely focused on me.

Finally getting the courage to do something other than stare at them, I slammed the door before they could make a move to get to me. I moved to the next door, throwing it open to find the same figure in the darkness, watching me.

"When one door closes, another opens. And I'll be on the other side of it, waiting for you." The figure spoke in a voice that was neither feminine nor masculine. I shuddered as I slammed the door shut in its face and took off down the dark hallway again.

"Only you." A strange yet familiar voice murmured in my ear, causing me to turn my head and stumble over my feet, a sharp cry of distress leaving my lips as my arms flailed about, finding no purchase as I crashed down onto my hands and knees with a pained grunt.

But when I looked up from my place on the floor, I was no longer in a dark empty hallway.

Students and professors alike watched me with a mixture of surprise and curiosity. A few offered me a hand up and asked if I was okay. I just blinked at them, trying to understand what had just happened, before mumbling my thanks and helping myself back to my feet. My hand flew to my forehead as I hurried down the hall, a mixture of embarrassment and utter bewilderment making heat spread through my body like wildfire.

I decided then that classes were officially done for me for the day. Instead, I kept my head down the entire time as I crossed campus and headed straight for the solace of my apartment.

Luckily for me, my roommate wasn't home. At least she wasn't in the common area when I made it back. I went straight to my bedroom and locked the door behind me, hoping that if she was in hers, she would at least stay there for a while. With my back pressed against the door, I closed my eyes and let out the breath I had been holding.

Letting my backpack slide down my arm and onto the floor, I moved to my bed and plopped down into the fluffy duvet, thankful for the opportunity to rest as I looked up at the ceiling and mused on what I had just experienced. I reasoned that I must have been seeing things. After all, I did have an early start to the day since I had to move my stuff in. Maybe I just needed more sleep.

As if the chill from before was still with me, I curled up in my blankets and told myself it was because I was cold, not because I was still scared and wanted to feel safe.

A picture frame I didn't remember having sat on my bedside table. Picking it up, I couldn't recall the photo inside it either. It was me with my mother; only the photo appeared to have been taken at some country club or something. My brows knit together as I brought it closer to get a second look. My mother and I would have never stepped foot in a country club, or anywhere this classy.

Glancing around the room, I realized there were many other photos of both my mother and me scattered about – pictures of us in front of places like the Eiffel Tower, the Leaning Tower of Pisa, and the Lincoln Monument. There was even a photo framed of us both throwing coins over our shoulders into the Fountain of Love in Rome.

There was no way any of this happened. My mother and I both worked hard, her working multiple jobs at times, so we definitely didn't have the time or money to go on extravagant trips like this. We always talked, more like joked about going to them someday, but I was more than happy with the weekend camping trips and day trips to the Falls we went to.

Our lives weren't perfect by any means, but they were ours, and we were happy. My mom did and would do anything for me, would sacrifice anything for me to be able to live a full life. She even tried to hide how bad things had been for a while, but as soon as I found out, that's when I got a job and started working to help her out.

Even though I knew others had it much, much worse financially, I knew how difficult it could be for a single mother to raise a child, and I wanted her to be as happy as I was. I didn't need summer vacations to other countries like other kids in my class had. I just needed *her*.

As I pondered and examined the images before me, my mind became increasingly clouded by my thoughts. I closed my eyes as a sharp, excruciating pain ran through my temples and across my forehead, causing me to buckle over in pain briefly. But just as quickly as it came, the pain vanished.

I placed the picture back down on my nightstand, making the decision to get back up, pull myself together, and head back out the door for the rest of my classes.

CHAPTER EIGHT

Xander

As luck would have it, Erik was standing in the corridor outside his room. Upon seeing me, he waved and came to meet me halfway.

"Did you see those things?" He asked, his gaze widening slightly despite his cool demeanour.

"Yeah, we were attacked, but we've recovered." Even as I said those words, I felt a twinge of guilt in my stomach as I remembered how far from recovered Avery truly was. "That's why I came to find you."

"It was weird. I saw them, but it was like they didn't see me at all. Or maybe they cared too little to notice me. Didn't stop them from scaring the fuck out of me, though." He laughed it off, but I could see a flicker of fear flash across his face as he spoke.

"Well, I'm glad you're fine now," I said, clapping him on the shoulder. "I hate to do this, but I have somewhere I need to be. I'll meet up with you and everyone later for drinks, though. We'll definitely need it."

He caught my arm to stop me, "Where are you going? I could come with you; I don't have anywhere I need to be."

"Just some things I need to take care of." Guilt crept up on me again as I looked at him. He was probably shaken from everything that happened and didn't want to be alone. But did I really want him with me while I stalked the Duke?

"Oh. Sure, okay," he said with a small nod, turning to head back toward his room.

I gave in. "You can come with me, just don't ask me questions and don't tell anyone, okay?"

His eyes glowed with excitement, and I laughed because he probably thought we were going to do something far more exciting than what we were really about to do. I led the way back to the gardens in search of Chaz because, even despite my bad luck earlier, I knew that was our best bet.

Erik surprisingly listened and asked no questions about what we were doing. He simply walked alongside me as if he hadn't a care in the world, but I knew him better than that.

The Duke was, unsurprisingly, precisely where I expected him to be. He and the Duchess sat beneath the white rose-covered gazebo in the palace gardens.

As we crept up to the rear of the gazebo, I raised my finger to my lips, silently commanding Erik to keep quiet and follow.

They were whispering to one another so quietly I could not make out a single word. After a few moments, Chaz stood abruptly and swiftly made his way toward the castle. After waiting a minute, we followed.

His blonde hair was easy to spot, so I made sure to keep a safe space between us so as to not appear too obvious in our pursuit. There were few places to hide in the garden, as it was extremely open, especially since he was returning through one of the more common routes.

Just when he was almost at the end of the path, he made a sharp turn. I picked up my pace to ensure I didn't lose him, and Erik followed my lead. Chaz stopped in front of one of the exterior walls, his head shot over in our direction, and I ducked behind a hedge, pulling Erik down with me.

Slowly peeking back over the hedge, I noted that he was gone, disappearing just like that.

Running over toward the wall where he had just been, I pressed my hands against the stone and examined the wall for something. For what? I did not know. There was no way he could have just disappeared from this area. Then again, those demons seemed able to do the same, so perhaps I shouldn't have been that surprised.

Erik huffed a sigh, leaning against the wall next to where I was searching. My ears picked up on a series of clicks, almost like the sound of a lock disengaging, before Erik's sudden yelp had my full attention. I took a large step forward as the wall behind him gave out, causing him to lose his balance and nearly topple backward into what appeared to be a dim corridor. Ushering him aside, I peered down the dark space and then back at Erik.

When he realized how much more intriguing this was about to get, he grinned mischievously.

"Come on." I pushed him into the corridor and stepped in seconds before it closed behind us.

"Now, *this* is interesting."

"We need to find the Duke. He could be anywhere down here."

Following the single tunnel, we were eventually met with a wider area with two narrow openings. "We could split up," he suggested as he shrugged one shoulder.

The passageway on the right was noticeably darker as the one on the left had a faint glimmer of light in the distance. There was a good chance that Chaz had some sort of lantern with him to help guide his way through the dark tunnels.

"This way." I jerked my head in the direction of the tunnel on the left before quickening my pace.

We hurried after the light ahead of us but were careful not to make too much noise. As we got closer, it vanished. I ran up to see how that was possible and cursed as Erik's footfalls echoed behind me. He bumped into my back as I came to an abrupt stop. Chaz had taken another tunnel that opened up to the right of me. It appeared as though he were contemplating his next move as he stood before several new openings.

Keeping a safe distance between us, I cautiously followed behind him after peering over the corner to see which way he was going.

I quickly lost count of the number of twists and turns we had taken, hoping he hadn't realized we were tailing him and making it impossible for us to find our way out. Then again, I didn't think he was that smart, either. However, after our fourth right turn in a row, I figured he was clueless as to where he was going, and we were all doomed to die down here.

After gods knew how long, and after losing all hope of leaving these tunnels alive, Chaz started climbing a set of old stone stairs that must have wound up many stories. We waited at the bottom of the steps for a minute before ascending after him.

Once we got to the top of the stairs, there was a single wooden door before us.

"He must be in there," I muttered, unsure whether I was even speaking to Erik or myself at that moment.

Pressing my ear to the door, I hoped I would be able to hear something. However, I was restless, and as much as I didn't want to walk right in and blow our cover, I did not want to lose sight of him either. My hand moved to grip the handle.

"Wait just a second. I know this door," Erik mumbled under his breath as I slowly opened it and stepped in. The room was dark, without a single light to be found. "Oh, shit," he breathed behind me.

"What? What is it?"

He gulped loudly before answering, "This is one of Amara's bed chambers."

A silent rage ignited in me for a moment before realizing that he meant the real Amara and not Avery. Even so, the bite of betrayal still stung.

"Right," I said through gritted teeth as I glared at him for a moment. "Well, why was he here? And more importantly, where did he go?"

The door behind us shut on its own, and a tapestry fell before it, concealing it from unknown eyes.

"He must have left. Maybe we should too."

"Whatever," I grunted, unsure if I was angrier with Erik or Chaz at that current moment.

As we approached the proper entrance doors to Amara's room, I listened closely once more. Not a single sound caught my attention from the other side. Though I had supposed if there were guards, they should not be making much noise anyways.

I opened the door more surely this time. Amara was my fiancé, which meant that even if guards were on the other side of the door, what could they possibly say to me? I was still the Crown Prince of Coldoria.

Luckily, as Erik and I stepped through, no one was on the other side of the doors. In fact, the entire corridor was empty. Perhaps it made sense since she was not in her bed chambers, but I still found it rather odd that not a single guard was nearby.

And neither was Chaz.

CHAPTER NINE

Amara

"I'm sorry, she was a *what?*"

"She was a Celestial, just like you and Avery. There is a reason we don't speak of her, and we didn't even long before magic was forgotten. You must be very careful with these books. They—" He paused, and I waited for him to continue. After several long moments, he finally did. "They changed her. She was gifted with the power of healing.

From a young age, she had incredible power, the likes of which we had never seen before. She worked and trained with the healers here in the castle, but before long, she was the one teaching them. Eventually, she became the castle's head healer, becoming stronger and more powerful over time. Of course, she used her powers to help everyone, both within the castle walls *and* all of Estrella."

Lawrence paused again, this time walking over to his side table. He opened the bottle of whiskey and poured two glasses. He walked back over to his desk and handed one of the glasses to me. I thanked him and took a sip, setting the glass back down as Lawrence tipped his back and emptied it into his mouth.

I had never seen him like this before. He was not one to usually show emotions. Still, something in his eyes and posture told me whatever he was about to say to me next had broken him.

"Soon, people from all over Soluna and across Caelestia came to see her with all variations of untreatable illnesses. She healed them all, but I believe that she began to crave more power over time. So, she started looking into dark magic. She wanted to learn how to take other celestials' powers for herself," he said, setting his glass atop his desk. "These books contain both light and dark spells, but do not give in to the call of the darkness. Liliana did, and she paid the ultimate price for it."

"When you say, 'the ultimate price,' what do you mean?" I asked with a shaky voice.

"I mean that the dark magic consumed her."

"What are the chances that she's still out there somewhere?" Even though I knew this was a sensitive subject, I had to ask. Liliana had suddenly shot to the top of my list of suspects. I doubted she was in the castle, but the idea of her stealing the powers of other celestials sounded all too familiar.

"She's gone. Because of this, you must be aware of the dangers and concentrate solely on the light. My belief is that you will become even more powerful in the future, and you will need to learn how to use that power safely."

He was clearly done talking about his sister, and I couldn't blame him for it. But I was more intrigued to learn more about Liliana from these books. Lawrence looked at me like he was expecting an answer, and I realized I must have stopped listening to him at some point.

"Pardon?"

"You should communicate with Calypso in your dreams to determine if she has any more information or advice that could be useful."

"And how am I supposed to do that?"

"Just reach out to her, and she will come to you," he replied as if that was obvious.

"Right," I mumbled as I walked out of Lawrence's office with the books he had given me.

I was a little too eager to dive into Liliana's books. I wanted to know more about my powers, everything I possibly could. With everything going on, I knew I would need to exercise my powers and learn how to properly wield them. But most of all, I wanted to know more about Liliana because

I had a nagging feeling that there was more to her story than what Lawrence knew.

Opening the book at the top of the pile, I began reading as I walked to my bed chambers. From what I had gathered, they were all books dedicated to healing magic. That would definitely be useful if I could actually perform these spells. Even though I had my powers for almost two years, there was still so much I did not know about them.

I'd never forget the day I received them.

Two years ago.

I still wasn't sure why or how it happened. It had been about a month, and it felt as if I hadn't slept once, my parents' screams echoing in my ears every time I closed my eyes. Even though it didn't feel real, the truth remained. They were dead.

No matter how hard I tried, I couldn't recall anything from that night, almost as if the events were encased in a veil of utter darkness. Whether it was my mind suppressing what had happened that night or something more sinister, I could not tell. All I knew was that their bodies were gone when the darkness lifted and their shouts ceased. And ever since, only the sounds of their screams remained in my mind.

I refused to leave my room since that night. Servants left food trays outside my door full of food I barely touched. I wouldn't let anyone in either. I didn't want to talk about it, and I wanted to be left alone.

A knock sounded at my door, and I ignored it as I continued to sob into my pillow.

"Princess Amara, this is highly inappropriate. You should be out speaking to your people and reassuring them that they are safe!" Prudence's shrill voice called just as the door handle rattled as she tried to open it.

"Inappropriate?" I scoffed at the irony. As if her behaviour was so appropriate. How could I possibly reassure anyone of their safety when I had no idea how this had happened? I definitely couldn't guarantee it wouldn't happen again. Most of all, I had been grieving the loss of my parents, so her words only made me... *angry*. I had always hated that woman, but what did she expect me to do? I had lost my parents. They were gone. *Dead.* I didn't want to see or speak to anyone, least of all her.

I screamed in utter rage as I thought about how much I despised her, and the end table next to my bed flew and slammed into the door Prudence had been attempting to open. I froze with my mouth agape, staring at the broken pieces of my table in front of the door.

The shaking on the door handle stopped for a moment before Prudence began hammering frantically on the door again.

"Princess, open this door immediately! Are you alright?" she asked as if she actually cared.

Muttering broke out on the other side of the door before it burst open. Several guards poured in with Prudence directly behind them. I remained silent, still in shock over what had just happened. If I didn't see the evidence of the broken table, I would have thought I'd imagined it.

I rubbed my eyes in disbelief. That wasn't possible.

"What happened? Are you alright? Is there an intruder? We have been on duty this entire time. How could this have happened?" The guards questioned me as they did a quick sweep around my room. Checking the balcony for some intruder I knew wouldn't be there.

"I'm fine," I whispered, unsure if they heard me as I was trying to tell myself that more than anyone else.

"*I am,*" Prudence interjected, correcting my use of the contraction. "What have I told you about speaking like a proper princess?"

I rolled my eyes. As if my grammar was really the most pressing thing right now.

"Get. *Out,*" I demanded.

"Your Highness." The guards bowed as they exited the room without another thought. But not Prudence. Of course, she didn't.

"You need to get out of this room. You are a princess *and* soon-to-be queen. You need to act as such." She lifted her chin, and her lip turned downward into that disapproving frown I was all too familiar with.

"You know what?" I breathed a laugh as I realized how much I liked the thought of something she had just said. "You are right. I will be queen, which means I am in charge, *not you.*" Her brows furrowed as I spoke. I got off my bed and stood straight as I took several slow steps toward her. *"You. Are.* Fired." I made sure not to use any contractions as I spoke those three words I had dreamed about for as long as I could remember, and a small smile pulled at the corner of my lips.

"You cannot fire me." She straightened as she spoke, her voice wavering slightly as her eyes shifted nervously.

"Oh, but I can. Guards!" I called, and they came running in. "Please escort Prudence here out of the castle grounds. She is no longer welcome." They did not flinch as they grabbed her by the arms and forced her out of my room.

She kicked, screamed, and flailed her arms as she tried and failed to fight them off her.

"How inappropriate and unprofessional," I called to her, sending her a small wave as she looked back over her shoulder at me as the guards practically dragged her out.

I sighed as I was left alone again, and the familiar screams of my parents replayed in my mind again. Squeezing my eyes shut, I fell to the ground and raked my hands through my hair as I tried to make it stop. *Make it stop. Please make it stop.* I begged my mind as tears began streaming down my shut eyes once more.

My door slammed shut, and the rest of my room began to shake. My eyes shot open. I thought it might have been an earthquake for a moment, but the floors and walls were completely unmoving. The furniture and fixtures, however, shook with the ferocity of one. Everything on my tables fell to the floor, and mirrors cracked as I looked around in horror.

"Stop!" I cried, and just like that, the room fell still.

Suddenly, I didn't want to be alone anymore. I wanted the one person I could always rely on and the only person I could say anything to.

Since my parents' deaths, he'd tried to see me every day, sometimes more than once. I didn't want to see him because he was right there with me when everything happened that night. But I needed him, and I knew he would help me figure out what was happening now.

Running out of my chambers and past my guards, I ignored them as they called out to me. They didn't try to stop me; they never did. They would just try to follow me like always, but I always managed to give them the slip.

Turning around the corner at the end of the corridor, I bumped right into Wesley.

I flung my arms around his neck, his hands on my waist to steady me. I pulled him in closer, and his hands tightened as we held each other. His one hand slid up my back and into my hair as he just held me silently. I pressed my head into his chest as I began sobbing.

Finally managing to stop my crying, I pulled away from Wesley, only to see all the moisture left behind on his shirt.

"Thank you," I said as I smiled softly up at him.

"For what?"

"For being my tissue." I pointed at his shirt, and he laughed.

"Gross." He pulled me in playfully, trying to wipe my face back in his shirt, and I pushed him back again. "What's wrong? Are you going somewhere?"

"I was only coming to find you. I needed to tell you something."

"I have something I wanted to tell you too, but only if you're ready. I know this must be hard for you, and I'm so sorry. You know I'm always here if you need anything."

"I know. I just don't want to talk about it, you know. I think I just need a distraction."

"Did you want to go first, then?" He asked.

"No, you go first," I insisted as I led him back to my room. I didn't know what he wanted to tell me, but I knew I didn't want anyone overhearing what I had to tell him.

I closed the door, and Wesley was sitting at the edge of my bed when I turned back. I sat beside him as I waited for him to tell me his news. He took in a deep breath, and I prepared myself for the worst.

"I made it into the royal guard." I couldn't help but jump on him. I knew how badly he wanted to join, and it had been a long time coming.

"I'm so happy for you," I said, but when I looked at him, I could tell he was trying to hide some of his excitement for my sake. "You are allowed to be happy and excited about this, and you should be. I'll get through this; I just need time."

"You will always love and miss them, but they will never be forgotten. And sure, that feeling of loss doesn't ever go away, but I promise it will get a little easier to cope with over time. Just remember that they would want you to live your life. A *full* life." Wesley pulled me into his arms again, and I knew he was right, but it was still so fresh. "So, what did you want to tell me?" he asked.

I needed a distraction, and I thought Wesley would be it, but I didn't want to ruin his happiness or excitement for what he had been working so hard and so long for. I was already going through so much, and I didn't want to burden him with something else. I would tell him, of course. Just not yet.

"Oh, I fired Prudence," I answered.

He laughed, "Did you really?"

"Yup," I replied with a tight smile.

"Good riddance."

"How did you find out you made it into the royal guard?" I wanted to take my mind off my parents and whatever had happened earlier.

"Well, they have been trying to recruit more people with what happened, and I guess I finally made the cut."

"Oh." *What happened* was that my parents died. I understood he wasn't trying to minimize the significance of it, even though he was probably trying to avoid bringing it up for my sake. It was still painful to hear it. "Congratulations."

"Are you okay?" His whisper was so low his voice nearly cracked.

"I'm doing better. I think. I just—I don't know."

"Do you need anything?"

A distraction. While staring into Wesley's eyes, it occurred to me what I truly wanted from him. Our eyes locked, and we slowly moved closer, but I couldn't deny him the happiness he deserved. He would give me everything and anything, and I knew I couldn't do the same for him in the long run.

I needed to be strong and grow up. I needed to do what my parents had wanted me to do, become who they wanted me to be. I couldn't bring them back, but I could do this for them. I could be the queen they always wanted me to be. I would learn what I needed to learn, do what was asked and proper for a queen, and, most of all, give up on the idea of marrying for love.

Even though I knew I had to marry Prince Xander, that did not mean I couldn't be with others behind closed doors. But

Wesley deserved more. He deserved the world, and I couldn't give that to him.

I turned away from him, "I think I just need to be alone." Now my heart broke for an entirely new reason. I wished I didn't have to say these words because I wanted the exact opposite. I wanted to pull him closer and never let him go.

"Okay." Wesley stood and walked toward the door. He glanced back at me before he opened the door, but I turned away and pulled the covers over my head. The door opened and closed again, and I waited a few seconds to ensure he had actually left. And then, I cried.

After a few minutes, I dried my eyes and told myself enough was enough. Like Wesley said, I had to be strong and live my life. So, I would do precisely that, just as my parents had wanted.

CHAPTER TEN

Avery

Present Day.

My new favourite spot to hang out was in the middle of the campus courtyard under the giant oak tree. It provided the ideal amount of shade and tranquility. The most beautifully crafted stone fountain stood a few feet in front of the tree. The sound of the water trickling from one tier down to the next made it all the more perfect. I had made it my routine to sit under the tree almost every day after classes were done, and this day was no different.

I pulled my eyes up from my book and caught the familiar gaze of Alec, the guy I kept unexpectedly running into, watching me as he threw a football back and forth with his friend. I quickly looked back to my book, but it was too late.

The next thing I knew, his tall, broad frame was before me providing even more shade than the tree I was under. He cleared his throat, and I rolled my eyes seconds before meeting his gaze.

"Can I help you?" I asked.

"I need you to wake up," his voice seemed to whisper.

"Excuse me?" My eyes narrowed.

"I said, did you want to join us?" He extended a hand to help me up, but I ignored it.

"Why would I want to do that?"

"Well, you seemed to be watching me for quite some time." He smirked and raised a brow as if he thought he had uncovered this big secret.

I huffed a laugh, "You were the one staring at me."

"So, you saw, did you?" He plopped down next to me and plucked the book out of my hands. *"From Steel and Stone. That sounds interesting."* He laughed as he flipped through the pages.

"It was until I was so rudely interrupted. Why did you really come over here?" I asked while trying and failing to snatch my book back, sighing irritably.

Suddenly, the fountain in front of us rushed to life and sprayed all over Alec, leaving him completely drenched as I burst out laughing. Several students stared at us in surprise. Clearly, the fountain's water pressure needed to be fixed or something, but I couldn't help but find amusement at how ridiculous he looked while I remained dry.

The corner of his mouth twitched as he watched me, "I was going to see if you were free tonight, but now, I think I could use a hug." He held his arms out as he took a step toward me. I shot up as I took several steps back from him.

"I'm good, and you can keep the book since it's ruined now anyway." My laughs carried back to him as I ran away.

I tapped my feet along to the soft sound of my music playing as I lounged in my room, scrolling through different social media feeds on my phone. I sighed as boredom crept in on me. I debated starting a new show or book, but I really wanted to know what happened in my ruined book. I went to the library yesterday to replace it, but there were no available copies.

Giggles sounded from the common area. *Meresay must be back from book club already.* She had been trying to get me to join since registration day, but I just hadn't been up for it yet.

A knock sounded, so I rolled off my bed and headed to my bedroom door. As soon as I opened it, I was met with Mer's smiling face.

"Our usual spot for book club wasn't available tonight. I hope you don't mind if we have it here. As always, you are welcome to join." She held up the book they must have been reading and wiggled it in front of my face.

Looking back into my room, I realized just how pathetic of a night I had planned and caved. "I guess I might as well join since you're all here anyways."

"Perfect! Go ahead and sit. I was just about to order takeout." She pushed my door open further, and I stepped out to join the rest of the group while my stomach growled in response. The pizza and wings that the group decided on couldn't get there fast enough.

For a book club, we didn't actually discuss the books very much. It started out that way but then led into a discussion of the male love interests and who we all preferred. To be honest, it was my kind of conversation. Fictional men were always better than reality. Eventually, the conversation slipped into who we would prefer for a partner. Most agreed on the morally grey type, even as I doubted any of us would actually be into a morally grey guy in the real world. But it was a fun fantasy, and like I said, real guys just didn't compare.

"Okay, Avery, your turn!" One of the girls giggled. "What is your perfect partner and ideal date?"

I thought about it as I took a big bite of my pizza and answered with food still in my mouth, "Definitely someone who doesn't want pineapple on their pizza." I crinkled my nose in disgust. The girls exchanged questioning looks with each other, but I continued. "He needs to love dogs and have a small close group of friends. Someone who likes being alone, enjoys stargazing, and isn't afraid to dance in the rain."

"Right... Good luck finding that in the real world." Mer laughed, and I sighed before taking another giant bite of my pizza.

The moon's light poured in through the window, and I got up to gaze at its glow. It was as if the stars winked at me in response.

"Only you." A soft voice whispered, making me turn back around. None of the group even noticed me as their conversations carried on. Figuring I imagined it, I turned back to the window and admired the silent beauty of the night.

"I think I'm going to go for a walk," I declared, grabbed my purse, then moved through the door before anyone could protest.

Humming to myself, I made my way to the courtyard. Not a single soul was out there. Tilting my head back, I stared up into the sky. It was even more beautiful now that I was out here. I began counting stars as I spun around, making it to about twenty before falling on my ass.

Folding my hands behind my head, I decided to just appreciate the stars instead of counting them this time.

Between the stars, a flash of ivy-covered wooden beams appeared above me. I rubbed my eyes in disbelief. One second later, they were gone, and rain began to fall.

The sound was soothing, so I didn't mind. Standing up, I decided to dance around in it. After all, if I wanted my ideal man to do it, I shouldn't be afraid to do it, either.

It was more therapeutic than I could have imagined — spinning, leaping, and splashing around in the puddles. I laughed as the light rain became more intense and the temperature dropped.

Lost in my little world, I spun into a hard body, strong hands catching my waist to steady me. I looked down and gasped as I took in my nightgown. My eyes shot up, meeting Alec's for a moment before taking in the rest of his appearance, from his burgundy button-up shirt to his black dress pants.

The rain pounded around us, lightning flashed, and thunder erupted, the sharp *crack* making me flinch.

"Avery, wake up!"

"What?" I asked as I looked back at him, only this time he was wearing a plain white t-shirt that was now completely see-through and a pair of soaked jeans. I glanced back down at myself to find I was back in my leggings and top. "What is happening?"

"It's just a storm. You've never seen rain and lightning before?" he teased, and I couldn't help but laugh.

The thunder and lightning stopped just as quickly as they began, and the light rainfall had returned once more.

"I have something for you," Alec said as he held up a shopping bag. "But I'm afraid if I show you now, this one will get ruined too."

"You got me a new book?"

"It's only fair. I did ruin your other one. Come on, I'll walk you back to your dorm." He held his arm out for me to take and escorted me back as he'd promised.

We stood before my door, and I thanked him quickly before running in. I waited until I was alone in my room before opening the bag. There it was, brand new.

I curled up in bed under my covers and opened it to the page I had left off days before.

A golden light gleamed around me, blinding me. What was this? Was I dead?

The light vanished as swiftly as it appeared, leaving me in complete darkness.

"Only you," A soft voice called to me.

A faint silver light glowed in the distance, and my feet immediately started moving toward it, unable to resist its allure. As I approached, I noticed a figure standing within, and as I looked closer, I noted that the light seemed to come from this person.

A woman with a face that resembled mine spoke as we stood alone. "Only you."

"Only me what?" I asked as my steps continued closer.

"Only you can save yourself," she said just as she began to fade into the darkness, taking her light with her.

"Save myself from what?" I demanded while reaching for her, but my hands were met with nothing but empty space.

She was gone. But her voice resounded in the darkness that engulfed me. "You may possess both, but you must work even harder for your light to shine through the shadows, for the moon does not produce its own light."

CHAPTER ELEVEN

Xander

Two years ago.

As horrible as it was, I had hoped that what had happened with the King and Queen of Soluna would have been reason enough to call off this ridiculous engagement. But father would not dream of it. He told me that if I kept disrespecting him, he would ship me off to live there until the wedding. I did not completely hate the idea of being away from him, but I would miss Hazel and my mother too much.

We were almost to Estrella, and I was looking forward to this short time away from him. He would only be here for the welcome feast, while Hazel, Erik, Victoria, and I would stay for the week. They had never been to the capital. I wasn't sure if they had been outside Coldoria, so this would be like a short vacation for us. We would pay our respects now that a month had passed and prove that our alliance and engagement were still strong.

With Princess Amara's parents gone, a part of me still held hope that she would call this off, even though I knew if she did, that father would somehow blame me for it and punish me. As if I had any control over what that psychotic princess did or did not do.

Hidden beneath my jacket, I still had bruises from the last time my father blamed me for something. *"You should be smarter. You should be stronger. This will make you stronger,"* he would say. He was a cruel, heartless king and an even crueler father. I despised him and don't know how I once believed he was anything other than that.

"There it is!" Vicky squealed as she pointed out the castle through the carriage window.

The three of them marveled at the lush greenery around us. Blue and gold roses, Soluna's national flowers, bloomed proudly on either side of the road that led to the castle grounds. Coldoria was always covered in thick snow, so they weren't used to this.

The ice sculptures that we were used to seeing in Coldoria were replaced by bushes that had been cut and shaped into different animals. Large stone fountains cascaded into one another, the trickle of water reaching us from several feet away as we stepped out of the carriage and into the main courtyard.

My father decided to bring one of his mistresses for the trip as if he would not bear a couple hours without one. Luckily, my mother had to take her own carriage, which I'm sure she preferred.

They stepped out of their separate carriages at the exact same moment. Seconds later, Solunian royal guards marched down the castle's steps. Following close behind them was the Lord Regent, Lawrence Le. Once they reached us, they all bowed, and father gave them a curt nod before they rose.

"Welcome to the Kingdom of Soluna," the Regent spoke. "I hope your travels were pleasant."

Father's only response was a grunt.

"Thank you so much for having us. I cannot speak for everyone; however, I can say that I quite enjoyed mine." Mother smiled, as graceful as ever.

"Splendid! Let us go inside, and I will have someone show you all to your chambers before dinner later." Lawrence gestured us in with his arms, and father led the way with the newest mistress on his arm.

The blatant contempt for my mother was getting ridiculous. How could he be so open and disrespectful? I do not know how I ever thought he was a good man.

I thought back to my childhood when things were good, and we were all happy, or so I had been led to believe. These things were perhaps less obvious to us as children. But when I spent time reflecting on it, I realized just how little awareness I had about the reality of the situation, not the pretty picture painted for me as a child. Once that realization hit, it was as if everything started to click into place in my mind.

There were so many instances when my father was busy with his meetings and would show up late when we had something planned as a family. Looking back now, I could recall how my mother's energy would shift if my father did eventually show, how her usual bright, beautiful smile would form into a tight line when he sidled up next to her. In blissful ignorance, I wouldn't have given it a second thought back then.

Once inside, we were brought to our rooms with Hazel, Erik, Victoria, and me on the same wing. The stunned looks on their faces spoke volumes as they fought to get a better look out of the small window next to us.

"Why don't you all go explore while I meet with the princess. There is no use in us *all* being miserable before dinner," I laughed.

"Great idea!" Hazel didn't wait another second before grabbing Erik and Victoria by their arms and racing back down the corridor.

Before the meeting, I immediately changed into more appropriate attire. Father would be furious if I was late, but even more so if I showed up in the same clothes I had been wearing when we arrived.

Once I finished buttoning up my dress shirt, I stepped back into the corridor and headed toward the designated room where I was slated to meet everyone.

Once I walked into the room, all eyes landed on me. Of course, I had been the last to arrive, which was just my luck. Princess Amara, who was chronically late, was already there, and I silently cursed her for choosing *now* to actually show up on time. I was not even late, and even though I avoided his gaze, I could still feel the glare that my father had aimed at me.

The last remaining empty seat was beside my mother and across from Princess Amara. I quickly took a seat while the Lord Regent moved to stand at the one-head table opposite my father.

"I would just like to take this opportunity to thank you all again for coming." He looked around the table at the few of us seated before he sat back down to continue. "I have brought with me the marriage contract for you to review and sign after dinner. You will see the details we previously discussed regarding the timeline outlined there. The wedding will be held exactly one month after Princess Amara's twenty-first birthday, and the coronation will occur exactly one month after that."

Lawrence slid the documents across the small wooden table to my father, who tried and failed to hide his smirk as he picked them up and examined them. It was no secret to me that he would be delighted to have a foothold in this kingdom in addition to ours.

And even though I would be King Consort of Soluna, I knew he would try to control me just as much as he did now. My eyes slid to Princess Amara across from me. Her head was held high as no emotions flickered on her face, which surprised me. Any other time we had discussed this, she either refused to show up or made snarky comments under her breath about how this wouldn't ever happen. But as I watched her now, I didn't see any of that. In fact, part of me had hoped that she would be able to get us out of this arrangement, so it was strange that she suddenly seemed all for it.

When she met my gaze, I arched a questioning brow, but she just gave me a blank look in return.

"I will look this over before our dinner and will send over my revisions before it is signed," my father said before standing up and practically knocking his chair over in the process. He did not wait for a reply before abruptly marching out of the room.

"Thank you." I nodded my head at Lawrence before taking my leave, wanting to get far away from both my father and this situation.

I knew about this arranged marriage for years, but it had never felt real until now. Yes, I wanted freedom from my father, but this wasn't how I wanted to do it.

I was sure I could bring Erik and Vic when I moved here, but what about Hazel? Our father had been trying to set her up with an arrangement of her own for so long. I had finally managed to get him to agree to stop if I went through with this, but a part of me knew that as soon as I was here, there would be nothing to stop him from doing it again.

I should find the others.

Figuring they would be outside exploring the grounds and really taking in the nature here in the kingdom, I headed outside first to find them.

We still had about an hour before we were required in the grand dining room, so I figured we would make the most of it. However, once my father left the kingdom, that would be when the real fun would begin.

I had planned for us to go travel into the heart of Estrella and see what it had to offer outside of the castle walls. My interest grew even more now that I knew we would be coming here much more over the next few years before my permanent stay.

Hazel and Vicky were in the gardens when I found them, clearly checking out some of the guards stationed there. I hid and watched as they made their way to a bench that sat a couple feet away from one of the guards, and their giggles carried to me as I crept up slowly behind them.

Behind the bench was a hedge, and I quickly moved behind it and crouched down, following along it as it led me to where the guard was standing. I peeked over the hedge and waited for Hazel and Vic to lose interest in the guard or become distracted by anything else.

I rolled my eyes at how long that actually took, finding it ridiculous that in a magnificent garden with beautiful fountains and lavish greenery, they had nothing better to look at than a *guard*.

Once their attention finally moved away from the guard, I whistled low so only he would be able to hear as I stood up over the hedge between us. He immediately turned toward me with his hand on the hilt of his sword. His eyes widened in recognition, and I raised a single finger to my lips in a silent command while jerking my head toward Hazel and Victoria.

He nodded, and I wasn't sure if he even understood my plan, but he knew I was there all the same, and I took this moment to crouch back down and head back toward the two of them.

Just as I was about to jump at them, I noticed a gardener further down my path. I quietly jogged over to them and asked to borrow the watering can they had in their hands, to which they obliged. I mumbled my thanks as I took it and returned to where Vicky and Hazel were seated.

I fought to keep my laughter silent as I raised the watering can above their heads and tilted it.

"Ugh! What the fuck!" one of them yelped, not knowing which one as I took off running as far away from them as I could get, my cackling drowning out the sounds of their shrieking.

Booking it back inside the castle, I ran back to where I thought our rooms were in an attempt to hide from their impending wrath.

All the corridors looked the same, but this one seemed slightly different. There were many more windows and doors than I remembered. Then again, I hadn't really paid too much attention before.

Erik stood in front of one of the doors, and I knew I had to be in the right wing.

"Erik!" I called out and ran to meet him, but when he turned to face me, I realized he wasn't alone. My brows tied together in confusion. "Princess Amara, what are you doing here?"

Erik's eyes widened as he whipped his head to face her. "*You're* Princess Amara?"

"Yes, and who exactly are you?" She asked as she gave him an odd look that I couldn't place, her cheeks flushing slightly as she ran her fingers through her hair.

"He is my attendant and best friend," I answered for him. "Now, if you'll excuse us. Erik, we need to hide out in your room for a bit."

"No!" they cried in unison as I reached for the door handle behind them.

"Uh—that is my room, actually," Amara stated.

Erik pulled me back down the way I came. "Come on, we can head to my room. I was just asking for directions in this maze of a castle. I didn't realize that she was the princess."

I was glad he got directions, as I was apparently lost. It did not take long to get back because it turned out that our rooms were closer to Princess Amara's bed chambers than I had realized.

Fantastic.

CHAPTER TWELVE

Amara

Present Day.

Avery still had no improvements or changes since she'd been in the infirmary. And while I anxiously waited, I'd gone through the books that Lawrence had given me, hoping for something more about his sister's healing magic, but so far, having no luck. After reading for what felt like hours, I took a quick break from the books to check on Avery again.

As I approached, I heard a soft voice from the other side of the door. I pressed my ear against it to hear better and could barely make out the sounds of a male's voice, speaking so low that it was practically a whisper. With a furrowed brow, I opened the door slowly to discover Xander sitting on a chair beside Avery's bed.

"I need you to wake up," he whispered.

The door behind me shut suddenly, and I flinched in response. As soon as Xander's gaze fell upon mine, he dropped her hand. I hadn't even realized he had been holding it until then. He stood up just as fast and headed toward the door as if planning to leave.

"Any changes?" I asked, deciding to ignore what had just happened.

He stopped, glancing back at Avery before looking back at me. "No."

"You should stay with her. I'll leave. I have somewhere to be. I just wanted to check on her first."

He nodded, stepping backward and moving to turn before shifting his attention back to me. "You really should watch out for Chaz. I followed him and found him snooping around in your room for the second time now. He shouldn't be trusted, even if he isn't behind all of this."

"Careful, Xander. I might think you actually care about me," I laughed.

"You? No. But…" His eyes flicked back to Avery, and I wondered what could have possibly happened between them within the month I'd been gone.

"He's probably just trying to dig up dirt on me, but… thank you."

"When I was with Avery, thinking she was you, I wondered if maybe the issue was that we just never bothered getting to know one another, that perhaps we didn't actually need to hate each other." His hand shot out in offering. "Truce?"

I considered his words briefly before taking his hand and shaking.

"I suppose that's fair. We don't have to become best friends, but you are right. We don't have to hate each other. You are helping me discover who's behind these attacks after all. And you may also be keeping one of my biggest secrets."

"I'm not the asshole you seem to think I am." His lip twitched at the corner, amusement glinting in his eyes.

"You still might be, but I guess I can try to get to know you better to know for sure."

To my surprise, he nodded in agreement, breathing a laugh before heading back to sit next to Avery. I took that as my cue to leave and headed back to meet with Lawrence.

Unsurprisingly, I found him in his office, thumbing through a pile of paperwork. He knew it was me considering no one else in the entire castle or kingdom would have entered his office without knocking. He gestured for me to sit in the chair in front of his desk while he finished reading whatever was in his hands.

Lawrence took the top paper from his hand and set it down before meeting my eyes.

"How are you doing?" He asked as if it wasn't a loaded question.

"The best I can, I suppose. What about you?"

"The same," he said, his smile tight.

"I've been thinking about a few things. Firstly, I don't know how much longer this barrier I made will hold, and secondly, I think we need to check on the rest of Estrella and Soluna. The demons may have attacked in other places. We haven't had any reports, but I want to be certain so we can figure out our next move."

"That is an excellent idea. We are still in lockdown, but I can send out a few of our best guards to scout." He turned to grab something off a shelf behind him and thumbed through what was likely a list of our best soldiers.

"I want to go!" I shouted, not expecting it to come out as loud as it did. Lawrence stopped what he was doing and spun back to face me.

"Are you sure that's a good idea?" He asked.

"Yes, I am sure. I want to test out my powers, and maybe I can help build another barrier or something," I answered, letting out a deep breath. "I just need to see it all for myself."

"If that's what you think is best." His smile did not reach his eyes as he turned back to the shelf again.

"If you are going, I will send double the number of guards." He flipped through pages in a binder he pulled from the shelf.

"It's fine. I don't want to risk pulling anyone from here in case of another attack. With us being on lockdown, we need as many people surrounding the perimeter anyways."

Lawrence gave me a wary look as I continued. "I'll be fine, I promise. Wesley and I left just the two of us and…." I trailed off as I realized just how *not* fine that had gone, but I still believed this was best.

"Alright. When would you like to leave?"

"As soon as possible," I stated with a single nod, leaving no room for negotiation.

"I will gather the guards and have them meet you out front in fifteen minutes."

"Perfect." I jumped up and practically ran back to my room.

After changing into more comfortable riding gear, I met the guards Lawrence had sent for me in front of the castle.

A pang of guilt struck me as I spotted my favourite horse waiting for me. The last time I rode her, I was with Wesley, heading out to find the prophecy.

What if I didn't get back in time? What if he never survived the attack when he pushed me through the barrier? My fingers absently brushed my lips at the memory of our kiss just before he pushed me through.

I had to be strong for Wesley and for my people. I needed to help them, and I needed to get back to save him. But first, I needed to do this.

Wesley's replacement, whom I learned was named Ben thanks to Lawrence, smiled at me before placing a small stool beside my horse. Using it, I stepped up and mounted my horse.

When the other guards turned to me, my only response was a nod. Ben rode next to me as we made our way through the front gates, the others forming a box around us.

We followed the main path that led into the capital, and I noticed that not many people were out, which was surprising.

There did not seem to be much damage, but I wanted to be sure. We first headed down all the main roads, spotting a few more people as we did so. As we passed by, the villagers bowed their heads. All in all, nothing seems out of the norm.

"I'm going to talk to some of the villagers," Ben stated before tugging back on his reins to halt his horse and quickly dismounting.

We stopped and watched as he walked over to a few of the villagers that stood several feet away, but could not hear what was said. But just as quickly as he had left, he returned, stepping up and tossing a leg over his saddle.

"None of them saw anything." We exchanged a puzzled expression before returning our attention to the villagers.

Did they only attack the castle?

We headed down some of the quieter streets and asked more questions to anyone we saw, but nobody knew or saw anything as far as I could tell.

After finally accepting that nothing had happened here, we headed back to the castle.

Ben leaned close and whispered, "Did those demons really only attack the castle?"

"I don't know."

I needed to report back to Lawrence. I wasn't expecting this at all. Of course, I was glad the rest of Soluna had not been attacked, but I didn't understand why that was the case. The demons had been after something, and I needed to find out what that was.

Lawrence and I decided to let the people of Soluna know about the attack and offer them protection and sanctuary within the capital. We sent more guards to patrol the village to ensure that anyone staying put would be safe.

Even though I was confident that the demons would continue to only pursue the inhabitants of the castle, I wanted people to have the option to leave if they wanted. However, if they did decide to go to another village or city, I knew they would not have proper protection.

Many people decided to stay where they were, but we did have a few that took up our offer to stay at the capital with the extra safety of the royal guard. I felt that being here at the castle was probably the worst place to be, but at least if they were in the capital, they were close by, and we could easily and quickly send more guards if needed.

While Lawrence diverted the attention of the castle's guards, I waited patiently outside the main gates. I did not want them to see me pouring my energy into the barrier as I worked to reinforce it.

After triple checking that I was alone, I closed my eyes and raised my arms. The books I'd read so far did not mention anything about light barriers, so I would be on my own with this one. I thought back to before and how I *needed* it to work. I needed to protect my people, and I would.

I let the sun's warmth wash over me as I focused on what I wanted to happen. Almost immediately, I felt the same heat radiating from within me. In every part of my body, I felt its familiar caress.

My eyes slowly opened as a golden light shone over me and expanded. The light shot up and seemed to glimmer into a glowing orb that encased the entire grounds. The light faded, but I could still feel it inside me, reassuring me that it was still there.

Surprised that it worked, I let out a laugh as the guards started making their way back to their posts around me. I moved to leave but lost my balance, and strong arms wrapped around me to keep me steady.

"Are you alright?" Ben asked as a flicker of tension crossed his face, and he quickly removed his arms from me.

"Yes, I'm alright. I must have tripped over something," I assured him, but as I took another step, my gaze blurred, and my thoughts became hazy.

"You don't look it. You're paler than usual and can hardly stand. Come on, let me take you to the infirmary."

"No!" I protested. "I just need to sit down and rest. I'll be fine."

His eyes were filled with doubt, "Should I take you back to your bed chambers to lie down?"

"Take me to the gardens. I think the fresh air will help better than anything else."

He escorted me toward the back of the castle, his hand on my elbow to keep me steady. I was already feeling better. I just felt tired, almost drained of energy. I did not think about what kind of effects the spell would have on me. It did not do anything like this last time, but I also didn't know if the barrier was as strong or large as last time.

We made it to the gardens, and he helped me sit underneath the same tree we had sat under before. I pulled out one of the grimoires Lawrence had given me from my satchel just as Ben sat down next to me, casting me a wary look.

"You sure you don't want to go get checked out at the infirmary?" he asked.

"Positive." The last thing I needed was for him or anyone to question why there were two of us there. "Thank you for helping me."

"It is my job," he stated before pulling out a journal and pen of his own, and he started humming to himself while he jotted things down.

For now, I focused on the grimoire, searching for anything that could help me strengthen my magic. *I should probably be working on my physical strength and combat as well while I was at it.* I needed to be prepared for when and if those demons, or anything else for that matter, came back.

This book was just as helpful as the rest, which meant it was not at all. All it had was more recipes and ingredients needed for various potions and elixirs for healing. I would probably just hand this over to the healers at the infirmary, as it would probably be more useful to them than to me.

I huffed out an irritated sigh.

"Is something the matter?" Ben cocked his head as his brows pulled together.

"I need to get stronger," I muttered, more to myself than him.

"If you'd like, I can help train you?" he offered as he placed his journal down.

"You would help me? Why?" I arched a brow.

"It's like you said; we are friends." He raised his chin as his smile beamed.

He and Avery were… friends? Was she friends with everyone here?

"Right," I said with a tight smile. The only friend I ever truly had was gone. Gods knew if he was okay. He was the one I trained with, laughed with, did anything and everything with, but now he was gone. I missed him. I *needed* him.

I rose from where I was seated, and Ben looked up at me, "You mean right now?"

"No time like the present. We were not doing much anyways." I shrugged a shoulder, and he instantly packed up his things and stood to follow me.

My back and arms ached as I lay on the stable floors, sweat and hay clinging to me as I panted. I had wanted to return to the stables to train so I could feel like a piece of Wesley was there with me. He would be the first to comment on how out of shape I had gotten, even though I still would have beaten him. He would say something like, *"Two years ago, you would have beaten me in half the time."* And to be fair, he would have been right.

Ben spoke, pulling me out of my daydream.

"I always heard that you were good, but I'd never experienced it firsthand. You're incredible. I think you should be the one training the guards, and me too, while you're at it." He grabbed his bottle of water and guzzled the rest of it down, then wiped the sweat from his forehead with the back of his hand.

"You are just saying that because you have to." I sat up as he leaned down to hand me my water, and I reached out and accepted it before polishing it off.

"I'm really not," he chuckled.

Ben sat next to me, and we began swapping stories of our past training. I left out some parts of Wesley and me. Some of them were just too close to us to share with anyone else. But I told Ben about how Wes was the one to teach me, how quickly I caught on, and how I surpassed him even more quickly.

"I never would have pictured it before. It's like every so often, I see a new side of you I never would have guessed at before. I guess that happens when you spend time getting to know someone, though."

"I suppose so."

"Well, you already know my true dream is to be a poet or writer, but I did enjoy the training when I was younger. I felt so much closer to my father. It was like he was there with me, watching over me as I trained and worked toward where I am now. My mother is so proud of me, and don't get me wrong, I am proud of myself. But I always wonder what would happen if I worked toward my own dreams instead. Would she still be proud of me? Would I be happy?" He bowed his head as he thought about his own questions.

"Are you not happy?" I asked, reaching out and gently placing a hand on his shoulder.

"I am, but sometimes I wonder if I could be happier. I am so honoured to be a part of the royal guard and would give my life to protect you. I shouldn't even be thinking these thoughts, let alone voicing them."

I barely knew him, but something about him pulled me in. He was like a hurt puppy that you just wanted to pull close and protect from the cruel world.

"Well, we do not have a royal poet. Perhaps you could be our first?" I suggested.

"I could not give up my duty to you and the guard." He pulled back.

"Perhaps we can find a way for you to do both, if that is what you want." I did not know why I was offering this kind of thing. In the past, I never would have held up a conversation with anyone other than Wes or Lawrence, but clearly, Avery was different.

I knew she was the one pretending to be me, but I was starting to realize that I could not just go back to how I was before. Maybe there was a reason why she was the way she was with other people. It reminded me of what Xander had said earlier, about how we never even bothered to get to know each other. And as I thought deeper about that, my face fell slightly.

Maybe I never really bothered to get to know *anyone*.

CHAPTER THIRTEEN

Avery

The next thing I knew, I was alone in my room again. Sitting at my desk with my book in hand. My eyes darted nervously around my room. I didn't know what I expected to happen, but I didn't know what to believe anymore.

Picking up my cell phone, I called my mom. It only rang twice before she answered.

"Hello, sweetie," she said cheerily through the other line.

"Hi, mom." I let out a long, heavy breath. I didn't even know what to say, but she just always had a way of calming me without even trying.

"I'm so glad you called. How are your classes?"

"They're fine."

"Is something wrong?" She always knew when something was bothering me... not that I was great at hiding it.

"I just wanted to hear your voice. I'm just…." Just what? I didn't know. "Stressed," I decided.

"Aw, honey. I know it can be a lot, but you know I'm always here if you need to talk about it. Hey, I have a great idea. How about me, you, and your father go out for brunch this weekend?" She suggested.

"Yeah, that would be— Wait. *What?*" I briefly lowered my phone and narrowed my gaze on it before returning it to my ear.

"What? What's happened? Avery?"

"I must not have heard you right."

"I suggested that me, you, and your father meet this weekend for brunch."

"Yeah, that's the part that confused me. I don't have a father."

"Don't say that. I know you are still angry with him for missing out on your move-in day, but he tried his best. He couldn't take time off work."

I didn't answer. *What the hell is she talking about?* I stood up from the desk chair I was sitting on and moved to sit on the edge of my bed. The pictures on my dresser began to ripple and change.

The pictures of my mother and I changed. There were three of us in all of them. Picking up the one on my nightstand, there was some man I didn't know with his arm wrapped around my shoulders, pulling me in. My face was scrunched up like I was pretending I didn't want him to do that, but there was a smile tugging at the corners of my mouth. My mom was on the other side of me laughing as she held her arm up high, probably taking this selfie of us. But I did not remember any of it.

I thought about Calypso's words again. *"Only you can save yourself."* But save myself from what?

Nothing made sense, and the more I attempted to recall the details of the images in front of me, the hazier my memory got.

My mom's voice shouted through my phone clutched in my hand. I pulled it back to my ear as she continued calling out to me.

"I'm fine. I'm just stressed. I'll see you both this weekend," I answered before hanging up the phone and dropping it on the floor.

Something didn't feel right, but I didn't know what it was. Was it me? This school? My life? I scanned my room for answers, but nothing came to me.

"Only you can save yourself." That voice seemed to replay in my mind over and over. What did it mean?

I stepped out of my room and into the common room, determined to find anything that could help me. Mer was sitting on the couch reading, her head jerking up the moment I walked in.

"Hey," she greeted.

She seemed different... *off.* At first, I couldn't place that either, and then I realized her face was almost blurry, as if it was a mirage and not a real face. I tried to think back to how she looked, but aside from her dark hair and green eyes, I just couldn't recall any details. Had I always seen her this way?

"Wh—what is happening?" The room around us began to blur as well.

A vicious smile was growing on her lips, and I could see it more clearly now. Finally, her face came into focus as the room darkened.

My eyes widened in disbelief. As she got closer, she stood in front of me. I felt like I was staring into a mirror. She folded her arms as she raised her chin and quirked a brow.

Her face looked identical to my own, the same mossy green eyes looking back at me. She had long, straight brownish-black hair, the only difference to my honey blonde.

She lunged at me, her hand raised, reaching for my throat. I screamed in horror, and she vanished, leaving behind a shadowy smoke that billowed around me. I stumbled back, and before I knew it, I was falling. My arms and legs flailed as my cries echoed around me. My heart hammered with anticipation, preparing to hit bottom. Hard.

But instead of landing how I would have expected after a fall like that, I was somehow standing completely still. Like I hadn't just been falling to my death.

The ground began to sway, and it appeared as though it were made of rope. With tears streaming down my face, I frantically gazed around me as buildings sprung up and surrounded me. I was standing on a tightrope, tens of thousands of feet in the air, and I found myself wobbling as I struggled to keep my balance.

A shrill snarl sounded from behind me. There were now wraith-like creatures heading straight for me. They clung to the shadows, almost as if they were cloaked in them, their blood-red eyes gleaming as they met mine in the darkness. I tried to scream, but nothing came out, my voice gone as my throat ached.

I wanted to curl up and continue to cry. What was happening? Frozen in fear, I tried to tell my legs to move, but they wouldn't. Desperate to survive, I managed to move my feet. Running across the rope, I completely disregarded my fear of heights, which was momentarily replaced by my fear of the creatures chasing me.

At the same moment, my foot touched the ground in front of me. The rope suddenly changed once more, and I was met with solid ground. Buildings morphed into trees as an eerie fog crept into the atmosphere. The creatures were relentless in their pursuit of me. Every time I chanced a look over my shoulder, more and more of them appeared.

Glancing back one more time was a mistake as I ran right into something, knocking me on my ass. A cliff that hadn't been there seconds ago stood before me, now encircling me. A wave of panic rushed in as I thought of what to do next. *Should I start climbing?* I was not a rock climber, that's for sure, but what choice did I have?

Reaching up to find a placement for my hand to pull myself up was useless. The rock crumbled in my fingers every time I tried.

"You may possess both, but you must work even harder for your light to shine through the shadows, for the moon does not produce its own light," That sweet voice sang to me again.

What does that mean?

The creatures closed in around me. I was going to die. This was it.

"No!" I cried, throwing my hands out in front of me, and a cool sensation washed over me.

A faint silvery-blue light glowed around my hands. Wide-eyed, I pulled them back to examine what the hell it was. When my eyes darted back to the creatures, they stopped their advances. It was only for a moment, but it definitely happened. I was certain.

Spreading my hands back toward the creatures, I put aside my doubts and fears. Concentrating on what I wanted to happen. What I *needed* to happen. I needed to survive. I needed to be stronger than my fears. I needed those creatures gone. I needed to go home.

A light blasted out, blinding me. Then, everything went dark. But this time, it was different. I opened my eyes and realized I was lying in a small bed in what looked like a hospital room.

I was pulled upright into a pair of strong arms. I stilled, unsure of who this person was or what had happened. Then my memories washed over me like a beautiful, warm rain shower. I pushed myself back, and our eyes met as we held one another at arm's length on the edge of the bed.

"Xander," I breathed.

"You're awake? You're really here?" His brows raised in disbelief as he continued to hold me.

"I-I think so." I still wasn't sure what had happened. My mind was still fogged over with shadows as I tried to piece together the memories of what was real and what wasn't. "You didn't wake me with a kiss or something, did you?"

"What? No, that's disgusting." His face scrunched as he shook his head slightly, finally dropping his arms.

"Oh."

"No, not you. Kissing you wouldn't be disgusting but kissing someone while they were unconscious... Who would do that?"

Oh, only some of the most 'romantic' fairy tales and cartoon movies.

"I dreamt about you," I changed the subject.

"Oh really? And was Dream Xander just as charming as I am?" His mouth quirked up on one side.

"Even more so."

"Oh yeah?" He leaned in closer.

"Well, it really wasn't that hard to beat," I laughed, and he actually let out a small chuckle himself.

He continued to inch closer, his eyes shifting from my eyes to my lips and back. A small smile pulled at my lips, and I closed my eyes, leaning in to meet him.

But before our mouths could meet, the door to the infirmary opened.

"Oh, my gods, you're awake!" Amara shouted from the door, and I flinched back.

My face warmed as I turned to face her. Amara's gaze swept over me, then darted to Xander.

"I'll be back in, I don't know, five, maybe ten minutes. I should probably get the healer and let Lawrence know you're awake." She flashed us a knowing look as she closed the door behind her.

"I guess I should probably—"

Xander cut me off with a fierce kiss, and my heart hammered out a faster rhythm in my chest. I let out a small sigh as all words and thoughts were forgotten. My hand reached up to caress his jawline before sliding around to the back of his neck. His fingers knotted in my hair as he pulled me closer, the pressure of his body warming me from the inside out. The kiss intensified as he claimed my mouth with his, and I desperately wanted more. Xander's other hand tightened possessively around my waist before he suddenly pulled away. Flushed, I watched him as I struggled to catch my breath.

"Still like Dream Xander more?" As his mouth tipped up, my fingers rose to touch my lips, already missing the feeling of his against them.

"Still a jerk?" I asked, trying to get my mind off what that kiss had done to me and what the absence of it was currently doing to me.

"If I wasn't at least a little bit of an ass, I don't think you'd like me very much." He shrugged as he put his hands in his pockets.

"Who's to say I like you at all?" My arms crossed my chest, and I narrowed my eyes at him.

Who am I kidding?

"You seemed to have liked me a hell of a lot a few seconds ago. Do you need me to remind you?" He leaned in again, his face tilting down toward me.

While I debated whether or not to stop him for the sake of argument, there was a knock at the door. As it opened, Amara, Lawrence, and a woman I didn't recognize entered the room.

The lady introduced herself as the head healer at the castle, and I only half paid attention as she explained all the tests that she was going to run on me. My mind was distracted as it kept drifting back to that kiss.

"Avery?"

The sound of my name had my attention returning to the healer, who was just standing there staring at me. In fact, *everyone's* eyes were on me, and I guessed they were waiting for me to answer a question I hadn't heard.

"Pardon?" I asked.

"How are you feeling?" She smiled politely.

"Oh. Um, I'm… fine." My cheeks heated as I tried, and failed, not to look Xander's way.

He hid a smirk behind his hand, but not before I noticed. "If you'll excuse me, I'll leave to let you run your tests."

He made it to the door without another glance, and I couldn't help but feel the sting of it.

Was I a bad kisser? Did my breath smell? I mean, probably, I'd been passed out for however long, and I doubt anyone brushed my teeth for me. Dammit.

Before he walked through the threshold, he said, "I'll see you later."

"I am sure you will," Amara mumbled. I shot her a death glare, to which she mimed the action of zipping her lips closed.

"Please lay back," the woman said while gently guiding me.

The name on her badge read *Midge*, and I was glad I didn't have to look stupid or rude by asking her it again.

After Midge was done with whatever tests she wanted to conduct, she recommended rest and taking things easy for a bit. As if I needed more rest after being in a coma, but then again, what did I know?

Then, Midge left the room, giving Lawrence, Amara, and me time to talk.

CHAPTER FOURTEEN

Amara

Avery told us about the dreams she had while she had been asleep, mentioning that everyone *except* me was featured there, but as someone else. Xander was a student named Alec, and Lawrence was the Chancellor at the university she attended. There was apparently a woman that looked identical to us, only she had dark brown hair. She said even though she looked like her, she knew it wasn't supposed to be me. As I thought about it more, it sounded a lot like Esmeray from the vision Calypso had shared with me.

"The shadow demons followed me in there too. I don't know if it was just a part of the dream or if any of it was real." Avery shivered as she wrapped her arms around herself. "Everything felt too real." She was still sitting on the bed while Lawrence and I sat on chairs next to her.

The fact that Esmeray and the shadow demons showed up while she was unconscious did not feel right. These demons were under her control, and I knew there were some demons out there much worse, locked inside the Shadow Lands. Was she working for the Shadow Lord?

"We definitely need to find a way to talk to Calypso," I suggested. She had to know something.

"Yeah, well, good luck getting anything out of her. She's always so *cryptic*," Avery huffed in annoyance, throwing her arms out in the air in a dramatic display of frustration.

"It *is* possible Calypso knows more about this sleeping curse you were under," Lawrence finally said. Up until that point, he had just sat in silence with his hand on his chin like he was thinking and analyzing every detail we shared. "I don't know how these healers could possibly be able to help us, but hopefully, this will never happen again."

"Sleeping curse?" Avery's eyes widened, "Like in *Sleeping Beauty?*"

"*Sleeping Beauty?*" Lawrence and I questioned in unison, and we shared a look before turning back to Avery.

"Never mind," she mumbled in return.

Lawrence stood from his chair abruptly and turned to us. "I should give you both some time alone. It's probably best if we keep Avery's presence a secret. At least until we can figure out what is happening. Amara," he turned to face me, "have you come to any conclusions with your investigation?"

"No. I have no idea who it could be," I lied. As crazy as it sounded, I had a nagging suspicion that Lawrence's sister Liliana was somehow involved in everything happening. I had no idea how it would be possible and no evidence that she was still alive, but it was a deep feeling in my gut that I knew I needed to explore. "As much as I hate to admit it, Xander may have been correct about Chaz. He may be behind this, and even if he is not, we should be cautious around him."

Lawrence nodded. "Alright. We must figure this out as quickly as possible."

"I know."

Lawrence moved through the door, leaving me alone with Avery, feeling slightly nervous. Even though we were identical, we were strangers to one another. And while I was certain that I wanted to get to know her, I wasn't sure where to begin.

"Aside from the sleeping curse, have you dreamed about the shadow demons before this?" This was an odd place to start, but I had dreams about them myself: the Shadow Lord, Esmeray, Calypso, and even Avery. Maybe she had too.

She cleared her throat before answering, her gaze fixed on her hands as she fidgeted with her fingers. "Yes, I've dreamed about them before. I had dreams of them attacking me in a dark decaying forest, of them talking with Shadow Lord. They've haunted my dreams ever since they tried to attack me in real life."

"I've dreamed about them, too," I whispered. Uncertain of whether Avery heard me, I continued, this time a little louder. "When I was trying to find the prophecy, I saw them attack you in a dungeon somewhere. Was... was that real?"

"Yes, in Coldoria, someone... or some*thing* attacked me. I was locked in a dungeon, and one of those things was there. Luckily, Ben found me and fought it off."

For some reason, that had my attention. "Do you find it strange that he found you? How did he know you were there?"

"I was supposed to meet him to go to the festival. He must have been looking for me for a while. I'm not really sure how long I was out before I woke up, but I guess he heard my screams and found me."

"Well, thank the gods," I breathed. Avery still hadn't looked up from her hands. This clearly still bothered her, and I couldn't blame her. I knew firsthand how horrible this situation was.

I took a deep breath, my eyes closing momentarily as I decided to share. "My best friend and traveling companion, Wesley, is trapped in the Shadow Lands."

"The Shadow Lands?" Avery's puzzled gaze met mine, and I nodded.

"It is where the Shadow Lord is. There were people there who were hiding from them. We wanted to save them and wanted to find a way for us all to leave that place, but Calypso said only *I* could leave." Tears burned my eyes as I fought to hold them back. "Wesley pushed me through the barrier as these other kinds of demons attacked us. He saved me. Time moves differently there, so I believe that he will be okay, but I need to save him."

Avery reached out to me but halted her movements for one moment before seemingly making a decision and drawing me into an awkward yet reassuring hug.

"We'll figure it out. We'll make sure Wesley's okay." I knew she could not promise me this, but it still comforted me all the same.

Avery and I snuck into my bed chambers through the old servants' passages that were no longer used regularly. However, many people still knew about their existence within the castle walls, so as we used them to travel back to my rooms, we were careful not to be seen. Once we made it to the door, I cracked it just slightly, peeking inside to ensure no servants… or anyone *else* was inside. After what Xander had said about Chaz snooping around again, I could not be too careful.

"So, which one of us is going to be you tomorrow?" Avery joked, making my lips lift into a smile.

"Maybe we should draw straws?"

"Are we going to have slumber parties now?" Avery asked as she held up a pillow like I was supposed to know what that meant.

My brow furrowed. "What is a slumber party?"

"You know, when two people hang out all hours of the night, have fun, eat snacks, and then sleep in the same bed." Once the pillow was returned to the bed, she leaped onto it, flinging her feet into the air.

"That sounds like something I would not do with my sister," I replied, and her cheeks instantly flushed. "That was a joke," I laughed, and she hesitated for a moment before joining in as I moved around to the other side of the bed. "Calypso had shown me a vision," I confessed, knowing we should probably try to figure out all we could. Maybe between what we both knew, we would get real answers. "It was of her and her sister, the first Celestials. She sent her power to a new pair of Celestial twins that shared the reincarnated soul of her sister." I shook my head. It sounded insane, but that had been happening a lot recently.

"She showed me that, too, in a dream. I didn't know it was a vision." Avery blew out a breath. "I've seen a lot of weird things in my dreams lately."

"It also mentioned something about the original goddesses that created Caelestia. If we cannot find anything on Celestials, maybe we should investigate the goddesses. It must be something of importance." A warm sensation filled me as I uttered the words, almost like a confirmation that I was on to something.

"Okay, so tomorrow, I will try to learn more about the original goddesses while you keep working on figuring out who could be behind the demon attack." Her voice was light as she lay back against her pillows. The healer had said she needed more rest. *Maybe I should let her get some sleep.*

Clapping my hands twice, the lights turned off. I rolled over, pulled the covers over myself, and then adjusted my pillow under my head. "We have a plan. Now we should get some sleep."

"I'm actually not tired. I know after being under a *sleeping* curse, it would make sense that I'd need *more sleep*," Avery chuckled to herself, and I turned to face her. It was dark, so I could only barely make out her silhouette. "Could you tell me about our birth parents?" she whispered softly.

I cleared my throat, unsure of where I should begin. "They were nice."

"Nice?" Avery scoffed. "That's it?"

"I loved them, and I knew they loved me. But they were busy ruling a kingdom. When I was younger, I wanted nothing more than to have their attention, whether it was good or bad. Now I understand the kind of pressure they were under. They did their best, and I know no matter what, they loved me. They loved *us*." I hoped that was enough for her right now. I knew she deserved to know more about them, but so did I. I still wished I had more time with them.

I could hear Avery's small, almost thoughtful hum before she spoke. "Back in my world, it was always just my mom and me; she was my best friend. We didn't always have a lot, but we always had each other. Every Friday night when I was younger, we would have a movie night, just the two of us, and we would rotate who got to pick the movie. Now that I look back at it, her choices were always something she knew I wanted to watch.

As I got older and lived on my own, it was hard for me to let anyone in. My mom was the only person I ever allowed to completely know me. My life was dull and mundane, and I liked it that way, so long as I had her. My life wasn't perfect, but I would have never chosen to change it. In the dream world, it was as if they tried to create what someone *else* would think was an ideal life.

There were pictures of my mom and me, and who I assumed they wanted me to believe was my father, going on extravagant trips and doing all these fantastic things. But that's not me, and that was not my life. It seemed like everyone else knew what they wanted in life but not me. I didn't have any unique talents or career dreams. For so long, I felt like a part of me was missing. But after being here for a while, I think I realized that this was it; this was the missing piece. I wouldn't choose to go back. I don't miss any part about it… except for my mom."

I could hear Avery's soft sniffle, which made something uncomfortable happen in my chest. "I am sorry you miss her, Avery. Hopefully, you will be able to see her soon."

The gods once lived in their own realm, and there was a god or goddess for everything. Sunna and Selene were the twin goddesses of day and night. When the sisters put their magic together, it was like no other. Even the other gods were in awe of their power.

Over time, some of the other gods grew wary and even jealous of the sisters' power. They did not like that when they were together, they were more powerful than the others, so they decided to place each sister under a sleeping curse.

While one was awake, the other must sleep.

Feeling betrayed by the other gods, the sisters knew they could not stay. They longed to be reunited in more than their dreams. They knew they would be together again if they left the realm of the gods, and so the sisters created their own magical world where they would one day be reunited.

In order to create this world, Sunna and Selene had to give up their physical forms. They watched over it, waiting for the day their souls would reincarnate in the bodies of another set of twins who would inherit their magical gifts.

With their magic, they made it so that their souls would be reincarnated into as many twin doppelgängers until their final wish could be granted.

Their spirits eventually underwent reincarnation, and while Cyra and Calypso spent some time together blissfully, it turned out that the prophecy wasn't about them. After Cyra passed, another set of twins would have the same opportunity 500 years later.

Calypso understood that Esmeray had always been a part of her, but she didn't know that Esmeray was her doppelgänger and shadow self. It explained why Esmeray had the gifts of the gods. Only, she used them for evil, giving into the darkness inside of her, using them to summon and raise demons with her powers.

Avery and I jolted up in bed at the same moment, our hands flying up to block the sun as it shined brightly through the window. I turned to Avery and found she was wearing the same stunned expression I felt.

"Did you dream about the original goddesses?" She whipped her head to face me. "Did it also mention a sleeping curse?"

"So, we both just saw that?" I asked, even though I had known the minute we awoke. I tried to process everything we had just learned. "Calypso and her sister were reincarnated from goddesses, and so were we. And what, they'll keep reincarnating until given some opportunity for their final wish to come true? What the fuck?"

My mind whirled with what this could mean. Was there another prophecy out there we needed to know about? Did this have anything to do with what was happening now, or was it a completely unrelated issue we would have to deal with? The words *shadow self* and *doppelgänger* kept repeating in my mind.

Avery groaned, moving down to hide under the covers again as I pushed myself out of bed to start getting ready to leave.

"We still need to know more, so we need to follow our plan. I will run and grab some books that you can read while I investigate. We cannot both be out just wandering around the castle grounds, so you… you will have to stay put."

"Fine by me, I am not a morning person," she returned, her voice muffled by all the blankets she had buried herself in. I couldn't help my grin as I finished getting dressed. Once I was ready, I closed the curtains and turned off the lights for Avery before heading out.

When I got to the library, I looked for books about Caelestia as a whole instead of just the kingdom of Soluna. I found a few books based on the different gods and goddesses and the god realms and hoped they would give us something to work with. I hoped that I would get lucky, and it would have some mention of this new prophecy and doppelgangers.

The lights in my room were on when I returned, and I could make out the sound of water running in the next room. Thankful she was already up, I left the books on the desk for her and slipped back out. But just as I was about to turn down the corridor, someone shouted my name.

"Amara!" I turned to find Ben running to catch up to me.

"Hi," I replied almost dismissively, not slowing my pace because I had places to be. But as I thought about that, I realized I was not even sure where those places were or what my plan was, and my steps stopped suddenly.

"Where are you headed?" he asked, finally catching up to me.

"To find you, actually." I figured he was high up in the royal guard. Maybe he would have known or seen something. "I am trying to figure out exactly what happened the day of the demon attack. Did you see anything?"

Ben cocked his head, eyes squinting as he tried to recall that day. "Nothing out of the ordinary, aside from the actual demons, of course. That wasn't our first time seeing them, but it was our first time seeing them in the castle. I can ask around and see if any other guards know anything?" he offered.

"Perfect!" I said a little too enthusiastically, but at least this was a plan. "You go ask around, and I will meet you in the stables later for more training."

I ran off down the corridor without giving him a second to reply. I decided then that my plan was to just wander around the castle grounds looking out for anything suspicious. It sounded easy enough. I could read more in Liliana's books for answers later. But now would be the perfect time to investigate while everyone was up and about.

As I passed by Lawrence's office, I did a double take, my gaze landing on Lord Chaz sneaking around it, looking awfully suspicious. As soon as he spotted me, he took off. Narrowing my eyes, I turned to follow him but ran right into someone else.

Xander stood before me, his eyes searching my face for answers to something I did not understand. My brow raised in question, but then it clicked. He was trying to figure out if I was me, Princess Amara, or if I was Avery.

"I am Amara. The *real* Amara," I barely breathed the last part, my gaze hunting for anyone who might have been eavesdropping.

"Right. I thought I was supposed to be the one tailing the Duke. Unless you think I was right after all?" His brow quirked, and I rolled my eyes as if I would ever admit that out loud.

"Well, I did not see you, and he was acting very suspicious, so I wanted to be sure he was not up to something." I dismissively waved my hand in the direction Chaz went.

"He is always up to something," Xander muttered.

"Now that, I can agree with."

"So where is… you know who?" He rubbed the back of his neck, and I fought to hide my smirk. Those two were so obvious.

"She is in my room. Why? Are you going to give up on your Chaz chase to go see her?"

"As much as I would love to do just that, more important things are happening right now. I'll let you get back to whatever you were doing before you found the Duke, and I will go find him."

I nodded my agreement, and we headed off in opposite directions.

CHAPTER FIFTEEN

Xander

The Duke was clearly nervous as he wandered through the grounds. I tried to keep a good distance, but it was becoming difficult. Every so often, he would check back over his shoulder anxiously, forcing me to quickly move behind any obstruction available so that he wouldn't spot me.

I had already guessed where he was going: the gardens, where he spent nearly all his time as far as I could tell. He headed down the main stairs, and I watched as he chose a door that led outside. I quickly followed and diverted to the left as he continued straight, trailing around until I found a safe cover to watch him from.

The Duchess of Caelia, Lady Vivian, was already sitting at the bistro table under the gazebo, tapping her nails impatiently as she waited for Chaz to join her. Once he made it to the steps, she stood while he bowed to her, taking her outstretched hand and placing a kiss on the backs of her fingers before she pulled it back.

They sat down and started discussing something, but I was too far away to make out anything they were saying.

Lady Vivian slammed her hand down on the table as she spoke, her voice noticeably louder now, but I could still not hear what words passed between them. However, only minutes later, whatever she had been angry about had apparently smoothed over as they sipped the steaming tea servants had set down in front of them.

I groaned at the thought of having to sit here and just watch the two of them on their date. I ran my hands down my face and then glanced at my watch, hoping it wouldn't go on too long. Huffing out a breath, I chose to wait it out. As I watched them talk and eat, my mind soon trailed back to Avery, and I wondered if I should plan something like this for her sometime. Sure, there had been a lot going on, but we both still needed to eat, right?

Eventually, Chaz stood, said his goodbyes, and headed back toward the castle. I waited a minute before following him, keeping to my side of the hedges as I ducked low.

Instead of taking one of the main entrances back inside, he moved toward a side door that led to the kitchens. For a moment, I thought he might have just been getting something to return to his date, but I shook that off, knowing that he would have had a servant fetch him whatever they needed.

There were servants hard at work preparing different meals for everyone within the castle. By the time I arrived, Chaz was already gone, and I was relieved to find only one door aside from the one I had entered through.

Suddenly, the door swung toward me as a servant carrying a platter walked straight into me. The look of utter shock that crossed their face as they realized who they almost walked into was quickly wiped away as they dropped to their knee and bowed.

"Your Highness," they said, face still down and so low I could have moved my foot an inch and touched their forehead.

Small murmurs broke out as the rest of the servants stopped what they were doing in recognition of me. They all bowed low, just as the first person had, and I'd forgotten they were waiting for me to either leave or tell them to return to their feet.

"You may all stand; just do not tell anyone I was here," I ran out the door, hoping I hadn't waited so long that I had lost Chaz completely.

Luckily, he was just around the corner. As I peered around, he was just standing there, his hand cupped around his ear as he pressed it against a wall. Bringing his other hand up, he knocked his knuckles against it, then moved a foot and knocked again. I watched him as he repeated this pattern down the length of the wall.

It took me a few moments of standing there, puzzled, before I understood what he was trying to do. Everyone in the kingdom knew about the not-so-secret servants' passageways. Of course, I already knew he had used some before, but his behaviour made it clear that he was searching for more, and something about the Duke's pursuit of them unsettled me. It made me think that maybe there were other secrets hidden within the castle walls.

"Xander!" Hazel shouted from behind me, making me jump in surprise.

Chaz whirled around, his eyes wide before they narrowed on me. I flashed him a smile, letting him know that I was on to him and that I wasn't the one who should be afraid in this situation.

He bolted down the hall, and as I went to follow, Hazel stepped into my path. I was met by her piercing gaze, her brow furrowing in protest as she stood there with her arms folded.

"Is this where you've been spending all your time?"

"What?"

"I haven't seen you in a while, and I find you here, sneaking around in random corridors." Her brow arched as she waited for my explanation.

"I was just... never mind. I don't have to explain myself to you," I huffed a laugh as I towered over her.

"No, but you should," she countered as she pretended to inspect her nails.

"Why?"

"Because I want to know," she answered, flipping her hair over her shoulder.

"You're just nosy." I rolled my eyes, fighting back against the grin pulling at my mouth. She was always like this. Even as a kid, she wanted to know everyone's business.

"Of course, I am," she giggled, not even attempting to deny it.

"What are *you* doing down here then?" It wasn't like most of us hung around by the servants' quarters and kitchens.

"I was hungry." She shrugged a shoulder as if it should be obvious.

"Well, now that you're here, I suppose I could use your help with something."

She placed her hands on her hips. "Only if you tell me what you were doing down here." Her foot tapped, waiting for an answer that wasn't coming.

"Forget it; I'll do it myself." I turned to leave, but she stopped me.

"I'm joking, Xan. Of course, I will help you."

CHAPTER SIXTEEN

Avery

My brain was fried. I had been sitting in the room for hours reading different books, hoping to find answers that I *did* not end up finding, and snacking on the various foods Amara had brought me earlier. I could recall when this would have been my dream—just lying in bed all day while stuffing my face and reading and to be fair, it still was. It was just *so* not my preferred reading material.

Glancing over at the stack of romance novels on the desk, I sighed. *Maybe just one chapter?* I thought to myself as I made my way over.

The hidden passageway door opened, and I flinched, my body freezing in place. Once I spotted Amara's face as she moved from behind the tapestry that hung over the doorway, I relaxed.

"Hey," she smiled as she tossed me something.

I struggled to catch it, and it slid right through my fingers, landing on the floor and rolling away from me. I bent over to pick up the now-bruised apple.

"Thanks," I replied, embarrassed by my lack of hand-eye coordination.

She snorted a laugh as she plopped herself on the bed.

"Any luck?" I asked, hoping her plan for the day went better than mine.

"Nope." She blew a stray hair out of her face. "You?"

"Nope." I threw myself down on the bed next to her.

"Great," she groaned. "I'm going to stay here for a little while, so feel free to go be me," she breathed, and I could read some bitterness in her tone.

If I was going to leave the room for a while, I figured I should probably clean myself up a little first. I went to the bathroom and turned the shower on, letting the hot water run for a few minutes, making a thick cloud of steam fill the room. I finally stepped into the glass shower and sighed at the feel of the hot water as it worked quickly to relieve my aching muscles.

After my shower, I towel-dried my hair and picked out something from Amara's enormous closet to wear. I went with a simple pair of leggings and a nice top, then grabbed a cardigan to throw over it.

Amara was already asleep in bed when I walked out of her closet, so I tip-toed my way to the main doors to leave, quietly closing the door behind me. No guards were stationed on either side of the doorway, but I noticed some walking back and forth along the corridor.

They bowed their heads and fisted their hands over their hearts as I passed, the same way they usually did. I dipped my chin slightly in return before continuing down the corridor.

Hazel stood in the great hall with Victoria and Erik, and my instinct was to go right to her. I had missed her, but I hesitated for a moment. I wasn't sure if Amara had seen her while I was cursed, so she was probably wondering where I'd been.

The moment Hazel noticed me, she started waving her hands enthusiastically, calling me over. I smiled in return, closing the space between us, and was immediately greeted by her flinging her arms out and pulling me into a tight hug.

"You're okay! I thought you were dead," she practically cried as she held me.

"What? Why would you think I was dead?" I pulled back, surprised by her claim.

"Why else would you be avoiding me?" She gave me an accusatory look as she placed one hand on her hip, clearly waiting for answers.

I couldn't help but snort a laugh at her dramatics, and her eyes only narrowed further, obviously still expecting me to answer for my disappearing act. Unfortunately for her, it only made my amusement grow.

"Oh, I missed you," I laughed again, pulling her back in for another hug.

Erik and Victoria eyed me warily, but I just shrugged them off.

"You wouldn't have to miss me if you didn't avoid me," Hazel countered, her voice muffled against my shoulder.

"I wasn't avoiding you; I was just... busy," I volleyed back, letting her go. It wasn't a lie. I *had* been busy. *Yeah, busy almost dying,* I thought to myself, but quickly shook it off. In reality, I didn't have a clue what that sleeping curse was or what it would have done to me.

"I will let it slide this time." She winked and then linked her arm with mine as she towed me away.

"Where are we going?" I asked, not that I was complaining about leaving the company of Erik and Victoria.

"You'll see." She wiggled her eyebrows, and I sighed. She was always so cryptic. Why was *everyone* so freaking cryptic?

As Hazel drew me outdoors, she pointed out the gardens as we proceeded. Since it was dinner time, I was not surprised that there weren't many people around. We followed along the trail for a short while before Hazel decided to go off it, guiding me to the pond hidden among the shrubs just behind the garden's main section.

The area was illuminated by fairy lights that swung from tree to tree. Lanterns lined a path toward the pond and even more floated on the water. As I looked closer, I spotted an open basket sat atop a blanket on the grass next to the pond.

"Is this a date?" I asked, turning to Hazel with a puzzled look.

"Obviously," she smirked. "Isn't it breathtaking?"

"Yes, it is. But why are you taking me on a date?"

"Oh, please. You're so not my type." She bumped me with her hip, and I stumbled a bit before catching myself.

"Then—" I started, but soon realized exactly what this was as Xander stepped into view. I couldn't take my eyes off him as he moved toward me from the same direction we had come. He stepped into my space, and it was as if he had stolen all my breath from me.

"You did this?" My voice was barely a whisper as I peered up into his eyes.

"With some help." He jerked his thumb back the way Hazel left, his lips curving upwards. "Are you hungry?"

"Starving," I answered, nearly cutting him off. He led me to the picnic blanket and held a hand out, helping me sit.

"Wow, how gentlemanly of you," I teased, and his smirk grew.

"I figured that since you made us pizza, it was my turn to provide the food. Wait… that *was* you who I had pizza with, right?" he joked, gently nudging me with his elbow.

I laughed, rolling my eyes. "Of course, that was me. If you don't know how to make something as easy as pizza, I highly doubt Amara does."

"I wouldn't exactly call it easy," he mumbled.

"So, what did you make?" I asked excitedly, reaching for the basket to peer inside, but he pulled it away from me before I could get a glimpse.

"I didn't *technically* make it, but I did bring it, so it still counts. Anyways, I just wanted to start fresh and get to know you… as Avery. Unless, of course, you have a triplet, and your name isn't actually Avery."

"You are such an idiot," I grinned as I pushed his shoulder. "Now show me what's in the basket!" I lunged for it but was too slow as he tugged it away again.

The snacks I had throughout the day in Amara's room were tasty but unsubstantial. My growling stomach was enough confirmation that I was starving, so when Xander opened the basket and took out chunks of bread, various fruits, and some pasta salad, my mouth watered almost immediately. I couldn't wait to dig in.

We ate in silence for a while, stealing glances at one another while we shoved spoonfuls of pasta into our mouths. *How romantic.* I snorted a laugh, and Xander's shoulders bounced with a knowing chuckle of his own. Once we finished with the pasta and bread, it was much easier to munch on the pieces of fruit while we chatted.

"Where were you? Why weren't you here?" Xander finally asked, cutting right through the casual banter.

"I would love to answer that, except I really only know the first half of that story. I grew up in another world, I guess." I mused on that for a moment. "It's actually pretty similar to this. I don't exactly know how to explain it other than it's a little more innovative. But as for the *why*... I'd love to know. Lawrence said it was to protect me, but I don't know...." I trailed off and then shoved a strawberry in my mouth, hoping to end this part of the conversation.

"What was your childhood like?" I questioned, hoping to shift the attention to him.

"You already know parts about my father. There are rumors of his infidelities and brutalities, and... they're all true," Xander answered flatly, like it didn't affect him in the slightest. "My mother is amazing, though. She always put Hazel and me first." My lips lifted slightly at the way his expression and tone shifted when he spoke about her. "She would read stories to us every night when we were kids. I think she would make most of them up as she went because Hazel and I always wanted to know what happened after the 'happily ever after,' so she'd tell us." His smile faltered slightly. "When I got older, that seemed like more of a sad dream. I gave up on the idea of love and happily ever afters for myself. But I still hoped that somehow they would both

165

find it." He let out a harsh breath, and I reached over and folded my hand over his in comfort.

"My mom, the one I grew up with in the other world, was my rock. She was my best friend, and I never thought I needed more. I avoided people and kept them at a distance. I still do, but since I've been here, it's getting easier to let my walls down. I thought it was because it was easier when I was pretending to be someone else, but I think it's more than that." I smiled softly, and his hand squeezed mine in response.

"Moms are the best. You must really miss her," Xander said, a slight frown pulling at his lips.

"I do. She is practically the only thing I miss from the world I grew up in. Things were always hard for her growing up, but she always made sure I was happy. She still puts my happiness above all else. She knew who Lawrence was. She told me to come here and even packed my bags for me. Was everything just a lie? She had to know something about this world, didn't she?"

"I can't answer that for you," Xander sighed. "Those are questions only she can answer, but I hope you can see her again soon. But it doesn't sound like any of it was a lie. You were her world, even though you were from another."

"Thank you," I said, leaning into his arms as he wrapped them around my shoulders.

We sat like that for a while, him just holding me in silence while we gazed up at the stars shining in the night sky.

As I laid in bed and read one of my romance books, I couldn't help but hum happily. I knew it was childish, and we had so much going on, but for one night, I just wanted to be happy and enjoy some romance, both on and *off* the page. I still had so many questions for Xander that I had chickened out of asking, but they could wait.

Amara had to head out for a bit, and it was starting to get late. I kept telling myself I'd read one more chapter and then go to sleep, but then there I was, four more chapters later, and it was just starting to get good.

The main door opened suddenly, making me flinch. My gaze shot up and met Amara's familiar green gaze, and I relaxed.

"We should really come up with some kind of system, like maybe a secret knock when it's one of us, so we don't have to hide," I suggested.

"Why would we knock? One, the guards would wonder why we were knocking to enter our own bed chambers, and two, it is everyone else besides us who should be knocking before they enter. If you hear the knock, that is when you should hide," she scoffed like that was obvious, and okay, maybe it was.

"You know who *didn't* knock before they entered? Erik."

I smiled smugly as a wince pulled over Amara's expression.

"Well, *that* should not be an issue anymore." She waved her hand dismissively before striding into her closet. She returned a minute later in a nightgown, and I watched her with raised brows, waiting for the explanation I wasn't getting.

"Not that I would know from firsthand experience, but in all the movies, sisters usually tell each other these kinds of things... so, spill!"

"What is a movie?" she asked, but I knew she was trying to avoid the question.

I flipped onto my stomach. "Not important. What *is* important is how that even happened in the first place. How long did it go on for? Oh my god. Did anything *else* happen?"

"You are so annoying," she said, but I could see the smile pulling at her lips as she tried to fight it off.

"Spill!" I repeated, throwing a pillow at her, only for her to swat it away like a fly.

"Fine." She rolled her eyes, then threw herself on the bed dramatically. I rolled over to face her while I waited for her to continue. "We met about two years ago. I couldn't be with the person I wanted, so when I met this attractive stranger in the castle, I took it as an opportunity. We did not know who the other was until Prince Xander caught us afterward. By then, it was too late, so we may have... kept things strictly

physical between us any time they would come to visit the castle. He knew there were no true feelings between Xander and I, so we thought there was no issue with it." She huffed out a breath. "There. That is the story. Are you happy?"

"Very," I laughed. "I can't believe you hooked up with *Erik.*"

Amara snorted in response, then immediately tried to cover it up with her hand over her mouth, which only made me laugh even more.

"Like I said, he was an attractive stranger, and I needed to let off some steam."

"By getting *steamy.*" I wiggled my shoulders and eyebrows at her, and she just rolled her eyes again in response. A beat later, a pillow smacked me in the face, and it took me a second to realize Amara had hit me with it. I pushed it from my face as I giggled, but at the same moment, Amara tried to pull it back.

The calm energy that washed through me the second our hands touched was like a cool rain shower. I pulled my hand back and exhaled hard. Similarly, Amara clutched the hand that had touched mine against her chest.

"Did you feel that?" I questioned in a breath.

"Yes, it was like a spark or a flame, lighting me up from the inside." As her mouth dipped, she ran a hand through her hair, her face etched with utter shock.

I made a face. "What? No, it was cold."

"What?" Her narrowed eyes met mine again.

I had a strange feeling inside as I held out both my hands between us. She looked down at them, hesitating for a moment, then took them in hers.

"What do you feel?" I asked, my grip tightening on hers.

"It feels warm," she replied.

"It feels cool to me."

Silver glow radiated around my hands at the exact same time that a golden light sparked around Amara's.

"This feels exactly like what defeated the shadow demons. It is the same golden light that I had produced all the other times. It was able to kill them the second they touched it." Amara's wide eyes looked around at the silver and golden lights surrounding each of us. "Only it feels stronger this time."

"That light can kill the shadow demons?" I jerked my chin toward the golden light that surrounded us.

"Yes. But it feels like it could do so much more than that."

"When I was under the sleeping curse, Calypso spoke to me. She mentioned how the moon could not produce its own light and that I needed to work even harder for my light to shine. She mentioned something about me having both. Maybe this is what she was talking about...." But I still didn't fully understand. My gaze darted around us, hoping the answers would just fall into my lap.

"Calypso's powers originally only worked at night, correct?" Amara asked.

"Yes." I nodded.

"And her sister Cyra's only worked during the day. If they were reincarnated from the sun and moon goddesses, then...." Amara stood abruptly, pacing back and forth in front of the bed. I noticed the way the lights around us dimmed as soon as our hands disconnected. They were still there but faint. "What if we are too? We all look identical. It sounds crazy, but it would make sense. Calypso said she passed her power 500 years into the future to a set of twins that would have her sister's reincarnated souls within them. That has to be us."

"But what does it mean?" I stood and gripped Amara's shoulders, trying to halt her pacing, but as soon as I touched her, we watched as water droplets danced in the air around us. My eyes grew wide in wonder as I watched them as they just hovered there, never falling. I pulled my hands back, and the droplets immediately splashed to the floor.

"Could you do that before?" Amara asked, keeping her distance this time. We had no idea what would happen if we touched again.

"No... before I came here, I couldn't do anything. But once I arrived in Soluna, I started hearing people's thoughts. I thought I was going insane at first...." I trailed off, my brows tying together. "Actually, now that I think about it, I haven't heard anyone's thoughts since I woke up from the curse."

"I have telekinesis," Amara confessed. "I've never been able to do anything else, but Calypso said we would grow stronger in our abilities, that we could obtain more. This is it, Avery. I think we need to explore them more." She grinned like she'd just solved all her problems with this.

"I don't know. I think we should be careful."

"We need to become stronger to save everyone. I *need* to save Wesley." Amara's tone was sad as her face fell.

"We will. We just should do it outside and away from people," I promised.

"Tomorrow?"

"Tomorrow." My chin dipped in agreement.

Tossing and turning for a good chunk of the night did nothing to help as my mind whirled with so many questions. Questions about my magic, the gods and goddesses… *Xander.* My eyes opened as I finally gave up on trying to fall back to sleep. And at that exact moment, my stomach decided to growl, and I groaned in defeat as I pushed myself up and out of bed.

I sighed, pulling on a sweater as the cool night air reached me. I wrote a quick note and laid it on the nightstand, just in case Amara woke up in the middle of the night as well. I didn't want to worry her.

Moving down the hallway, I nodded at the guards on duty as I passed them and made my way toward the kitchens.

When I swung the door open, I came face to face with Xander, who stood in the centre of the kitchen, leaning against the island.

"Did you also sneak off for a late-night snack?" I teased. He jumped at the sound of my voice, clearly not hearing me enter.

"Guilty," he answered as he raised his hands in the air, and a boyish grin pulled at his lips—lips that I stared at for far longer than necessary as I remembered how they felt against mine.

Rifling through the fridge, I found a tub of icing. *Jackpot.* I opened it up and grabbed two spoons from the utensil drawer. I offered one to Xander, and he accepted it with a quirk of one brow. I didn't waste any time sticking the spoon in and taking a big, greedy spoonful of vanilla icing.

"Perhaps next time I will just bring icing on our date," he laughed, dipping his own spoon in.

"So, it *was* a date?" I knew I joked about it being one to Hazel, but he didn't technically ever ask me to go on a date.

"Of course, it was. At least, it was to me. Did you not want it to be?"

"I did want that. I just wasn't sure if you did." I avoided meeting his gaze. I hated having to admit my feelings to people and usually always avoided having to. It made me nervous, not knowing if it was reciprocated. But then it hit me that I could listen in on what he was thinking. Sure, it was cheating, but I was desperate to know how he felt.

"Why wouldn't she be sure?"

I continued, "It's just that… I wasn't sure if anything had happened while I was asleep, and then we kissed, and we hadn't kissed since, and I wasn't sure if you kissed me when I woke up because it was just a weird impulse. I wasn't sure if you regretted it. But then you set up the picnic for us for our first date. So, I wasn't sure if it was an actual date or something else, and *oh my god,* I'm rambling." I finally managed to shut myself up, slapping my hand over my mouth as my cheeks heated from embarrassment.

"You're wrong," was all he said.

"About which part?" Considering I had already forgotten half of what I had blabbered on about, there was a lot I could have been wrong about.

"The part about it being our first date. I actually consider this to be our first date location." He gestured around the room.

"The kitchens?" I asked in disbelief.

"Don't you remember?" He inched closer.

"When we made pizza?"

He nodded.

"Well, some date that was. You ran out of here all in a huff with no explanation." I crossed my arms as I pinned him with my gaze, silently demanding an answer.

"Well, I didn't know you were you. I was confused and conflicted about the growing feelings I had for you. And then I remembered that you, well, not *you*, but who I thought was you at the time, had been sleeping with Erik, and I got jealous and… just couldn't handle it."

"Clearly," I rolled my eyes. I guessed he had a point, but it was still incredibly rude.

"I'm sorry. But like I said on our picnic, I want to start fresh and get to know *Avery*, not Avery pretending to be Amara."

Xander walked me back to my room, and I could no longer suppress the yawns that kept calling me back to bed. When we arrived at my door, he gave me a gentle kiss on the cheek and left without another word.

CHAPTER SEVENTEEN

Avery

When I awoke the following morning, Amara was already gone. She left a note on my bedside table, letting me know she'd be meeting with Lawrence to discuss some political matters and that I should be okay to leave the room for a bit if I wanted. She had also mentioned meeting me later by the stables to practice our magic but didn't note an actual time.

Stretching and letting out a loud, obnoxious sigh, I rolled out of bed and quickly got ready for the day. Once I was all set, I moved toward the door. But before I could even grip the handle, it opened before me.

I caught sight of Chaz as he was about to step over the threshold, my small gasp causing him to freeze as his gaze landed on me.

I crossed my arms and glared, blocking his way in. "What do you think you're doing entering my bed chambers?"

"I— I thought you were in meetings today," he stammered out his poor attempt at an excuse, his shock still etched into his expression.

"So… you what? Thought you would just snoop through my chambers?" My eyes narrowed further as I debated calling for Amara's guards or not.

He stepped back, holding his arms up defensively in front of him. "Of course not," he sneered. "I was…" He glanced around as he fought to find a better excuse, but I already knew what he was doing. Amara had already filled me in on what Xander had told her. "I was going to ask if Vivian could borrow a hat."

"A hat?" I balked.

"Yes, but I just remembered you have terrible taste, so that would not do." He turned and high-tailed it down the corridor. I watched him until he disappeared around a corner to ensure he was gone for good and wasn't just going to turn around and come right back.

We had fewer guards stationed in this wing to reduce the likelihood of someone spotting us together, but perhaps we had gotten rid of too many. We knew Chaz was up to something and couldn't be trusted. I didn't feel safe knowing that he could just show up in our room at any point.

Ben rounded the corner with two other guards, and I grinned. I waved my arm to get his attention, and he came over and greeted me.

"Are you heading somewhere?" he asked.

"Just trying to find something to do," I admitted, shrugging a shoulder.

He cocked his head slightly, "I thought you had meetings all day?"

Did everyone know about these meetings?

"Cancelled," I said, hoping that he, *or Chaz,* wouldn't think too much about it.

"Well, we could go read," Ben suggested. "Or we could go train some more?"

"Training...." I drawled out as more of a question, but he took it as an answer as he dipped his chin in agreement.

"Training it is."

As I thought about it, I guessed it wouldn't be the worst idea in the world. I was lazy and had little to no physical strength, so it wasn't like I couldn't use the conditioning. I figured that Amara just wanted to be prepared, and if that was the case, then so did I.

Ben led me out toward the stables, and I hoped he would be long gone by the time Amara came around here looking for me to do our own training. If not, I'd let her be the one to explain it to him.

I expected it to rain any moment as the sky steadily darkened and a cool chill filled the air. I was glad, as that usually meant there would likely be fewer people out and about if it did.

I always loved the rain. My mother always said, "Why wait for the storm to pass when you can dance in the rain?" I knew she didn't make that up herself, but I loved it all the same. Whenever it rained when I was younger, we would run outside on the front driveway and dance in the rain. Even in high school, it was always something we would do together.

I smiled at the memories of dancing with my mom in the cool rain, jumping around in puddles, and splashing each other. I spun around as I held my hands out, laughing as I envisioned being there now and doing just that.

A cold, wet droplet splashed against my cheek. Then another, and another. I opened my eyes and tilted my head back as the clouds darkened and water began to pour around me.

"What are you doing?" Ben asked, grabbing my hand with his and trying to pull me into the stables and out of the rain.

"I'm not waiting for the storm to pass," I laughed as my arms flew out, taking advantage of the moment to dance and jump around in the rain.

He watched me warily, his eyes darting back and forth between me and the dry stable.

"Live a little!" I shouted as thunder rumbled overhead.

I grabbed Ben's hand, trying to twirl him around. He finally caved and danced around with me, his smile all but brightening the darkness from the storm clouds. We continued dancing and jumping in the muddy rain puddles.

Ben even did a cartwheel. I attempted one but fell right on my ass into a giant puddle. He paused for a moment, worry etching into his face before I broke out into hysterical laughter, and he joined in again.

"I used to always do this with my mom," I said without realizing it.

"Really? I cannot picture the Queen doing this." He gestured around to the mess we were covered in.

"Right, what I meant to say, was I used to always *wish* my mom would do this with me."

He gave me a sad smile, and I wondered if he had done things like this with his dad before he passed away. The way I had to convince him to join me initially made me think that wasn't the case.

He held out a hand for me to take. "Shall we get out of the rain now?"

"I guess," I replied, taking his hand and allowing him to help me to my feet.

We walked into the stables, and Ben handed me a towel. I didn't know why there were even towels inside the stables, but considering I knew absolutely nothing about stables or horses, I just shrugged it off and accepted it.

Ben tossed me a wooden sword half a second before he lunged at me with another. I barely had time to toss my towel to the ground and duck out of the way.

"What the fuck?" I screamed, arms up and taking several steps away from him. *Has he gone mad?*

His brows furrowed as his head tilted. "I thought you said you wanted to train, so I figured we'd start with sparring."

"I don't know anything about sparring!"

He shook his head and chuckled. "Uh-huh. You're hilarious." Within the next breath, he swung at me again.

I screamed again as I jumped and hid behind a hay bale.

"What are you doing?" He asked.

"I thought we would do, like, push-ups or some cardio. I didn't think you would go all *Inigo Montoya* on me!"

"Huh?" Ben crouched down so that we were at eye level as I continued to hide behind the hay. "We could do something else if you'd prefer. I just figured you'd want to spar again."

"I've forgotten how," I said, unsure what other excuse I could give.

"You don't just forget something like that, especially with your skills."

"Okay, so let's pretend I had no skills. Teach me," I offered.

"But why?"

"For other training purposes," I waved my hand dismissively. That made zero sense, but hopefully, he wouldn't question me on it.

"Alright." He rubbed the back of his neck as confusion washed over him again. It was gone a second later, and he helped me back up. "So, you want me to train you?"

"Yes." I nodded.

He bent over, picked up the sword I threw when I dove for the hay and handed it back to me.

"Thank you," I murmured, my cheeks flushing with embarrassment.

Ben showed me how to correctly hold the sword first. He said it was important to have a comfortable yet firm grip. Then, he taught me footwork, emphasizing how essential it was to master my footwork before ever so much as holding a sword in my hand.

After I had a basic understanding of the footwork, he showed me a few different stances and positions to try. He would call different names or moves for me to counter, and with each, I failed miserably.

As if it couldn't get any more embarrassing, Xander found us and watched as he leaned against a wall. I didn't have to look his way. I already knew his gaze was fixed on me, and I could feel the heat of it in everything I did. I was already bad enough before he showed up, but now I was somehow even worse.

Xander's steps caught my attention, and I sent a silent prayer up to whatever gods were listening that he decided to leave, but of course, he did not. The sound of his footfalls grew nearer, the audible crunching of hay and sticks causing me to completely lose focus.

Ben swung the sword at me, and I stumbled back... right into the arms of Xander.

"Need a hand?" he whispered, the brush of his lips against the shell of my ear causing a warmth to spread throughout my body. Then he let me go, and I felt the absence of his hands almost immediately. But before I could do or say anything other than stare at him with my mouth open, he took the sword from my hand and faced Ben. "Come on then, *Brent.*"

I rolled my eyes but accepted the chance to sit and watch while quenching my thirst with some water.

Ben didn't call out any terms as he and Xander faced off. The way their feet danced around and swords clashed was actually kind of beautiful. I shuddered to think about what it would look like if they were actually trying to kill each other.

Xander was about to land a blow on Ben, but he blocked it at the last moment. Xander only smirked before spinning around and trying another attack. They kept going on and on for a while until, eventually, I got so bored I had to hide a yawn behind my hand.

"Enough!" I called, finally standing back up from my seat on the haystack and making my way back toward them. "I thought this was about training me?" I crossed my arms and gave them both a pointed look.

Ben cleared his throat and bowed, "Of course, I apologize."

"No need to apologize. Let's just get back to training." I tried to take my sword back from Xander, but he took a step back, giving me a taunting grin as he held the sword slightly out of my reach. "Seriously?"

"Why don't I train you for a bit?" he suggested.

"Because you make me even more nervous," I blurted, covering my hand over my mouth, hoping that I could somehow take it back.

"Oh, really?" This time Xander took several steps closer, closing the distance between us, and I had to tip my head back to meet his heated gaze.

"He is actually quite good. To be honest, if you didn't intervene, I think he would have won," Ben admitted. Xander gave him a once over and smiled.

"You're not too bad yourself, Ben." I almost flinched in surprise at the use of his real name.

"I'll leave you to it," Ben bowed again before leaving us alone.

"Here, let me show you how to *properly* hold and use a sword," Xander said, stepping so close that I could feel the warmth of his body.

I lifted my chin and turned my head back, expecting him to be directly behind me to help me hold my sword. But instead, he was standing there with his sword in hand, watching me like he was waiting for me to do something.

"I thought you were going to show me how to properly use this thing?" I waved the wooden sword in the air for emphasis.

"I am; I was just waiting to make sure you were ready," He eyed me again, and his eyebrows furrowed slightly.

"I was expecting you to, I don't know, come up behind me and guide my hands with yours along the sword." My cheeks warmed, and I looked to my feet, realizing how stupid that was.

He stepped closer. "Why would I do that?"

"That's what they always do in the movies," I muttered.

"Is that what they do where you grew up?"

"Well, no... maybe... I don't really know. We don't really fight with swords where I'm from. I mean, there's fencing, but I think that's more for fun... or something." I continued to keep my gaze fixed on the ground as I lightly kicked the dirt around my feet, my embarrassment only growing.

Xander's fingers gently lifted my chin, and I caught the hint of a smirk tugging at his lips before raising my eyes to meet his at last. "Was this just an excuse you came up with for me to touch you?"

"What?" I gasped, jerking away from him as the shock of his question practically sent me into a coughing fit. I could

feel my cheeks flush with heat, and as I spotted his smirk, I had no doubts that they were bright pink.

"I'm joking," He let out a laugh. "Or maybe I'm not." He shrugged a shoulder, and his grin grew, not even trying to hide it.

All I could do was watch as he took a step closer. He came up behind me and slowly glided his fingers down my arms, then wrapped them firmly around mine, tightening my grip on my practice sword. He raised our arms, holding the sword out in front of me. Xander moved even closer, pressing his chest flush against my back. My breaths seemed to quicken, and I glanced over my shoulder at him.

"Is this what you wanted?" His head lowered as he whispered in my ear.

"Maybe," I breathed.

"Well, it's not very practical." He laughed as he pulled away, and I immediately missed the warmth of his body pressed against mine.

"Right," I clipped out in return, my smile pressed into a tight line.

Xander continued to show me the same things I had already gone over earlier with Ben. And somehow, I was even worse than before. I wasn't sure if it was because I'd been at it for a while and exhaustion was setting in, or because I was too damn nervous around Xander. As I admired how he looked with damp hair and tiny beads of sweat above his brow, I knew exactly which answer was the biggest contributing factor.

It was the latter. *Definitely* the latter.

CHAPTER EIGHTEEN

Amara

The meetings with Lawrence were boring, as usual. I only half paid attention, taking more notice of how he had been acting than anything that was said. Lawrence had been so fidgety the entire time — pulling at the collar of his shirt, adjusting the tightness of his tie, and pushing up his glasses. It was so unlike him that I just knew something was bothering him.

After the other few attendees had left, I stayed behind. The conference room we used was not very large. I sat at the head of the table with Lawrence to my right. Besides the tables and chairs, the room was empty. A single window sat behind me, and the rest of the walls were a plain, boring beige. Not a single decoration or picture was hung anywhere. It was as if they wanted these meetings to be as dull as possible.

"What is bothering you?" I asked Lawrence after he finished gathering all the papers and stacking them into a neat pile.

He glanced at the door, then back to me, placing his finger over his lips in a silent command.

"Just your everyday stresses, nothing for you to worry about, Your Highness." He tilted his head down and gave me a look over his glasses.

"Of course," I said before mouthing, 'your office?' and he nodded. "Allow me to accompany you back to your office," I insisted.

We silently made our way to Lawrence's office, not speaking a single word along the way. Every guard we passed bowed their heads, and I took note of all their faces. We did not know who we could trust anymore.

Lawrence unlocked the door to his office and held it open for me as I walked through. He cautiously looked around the corridor before stepping in and locking it.

Instead of taking his usual seat, Lawrence went over to a side table. He pressed a button on a radio that I didn't remember seeing before, and music began playing. Then, he made his way to his chair on the other side of his desk.

"What is happening?" I asked, keeping my voice low.

"Just a precaution. I think whoever is behind this must have some sort of rank or title. They must know the layout of this castle well, and we do not know who we can trust anymore." He adjusted his tie nervously again, and I glanced at the door, half expecting this big, bad person to burst in.

"That would make sense, but I still do not have any real leads. Maybe Xander is right that it is Chaz. But it almost seems too obvious." I shook my head, raking my fingers through my hair.

"We will figure this out," he promised, and I nodded my agreement even though I knew there was a good chance we would not.

"I need to go find Avery. We are going to work on our powers, and hopefully, they can help." I pushed my chair back and stood, feeling all the blood rush to my head as my balance was thrown off. I stumbled as I attempted to step toward the door.

Lawrence rose, his chair knocking over as he rushed to help me. "Are you alright?" he asked, his face pinched with concern as he placed a hand on my shoulder.

"I am fine. I think I just stood too quickly. I should probably also eat something." Lawrence helped me back into the chair. He grabbed a scone from his coffee cart and handed it to me.

I accepted it with shaky hands and mumbled my thanks as I took a bite, realizing this was the first thing I had eaten in several hours. As I took another bite, my stomach groaned with pleasure, and I eyed the rest sitting on the cart. Lawrence noticed my gaze and brought me the plate with the rest of the scones.

"Do you have something I could carry these in? Perhaps I should bring some to Avery as well. I don't know if she has eaten much today either," I said, covering my mouth as I chewed and swallowed.

"Of course." He reached for a basket below the coffee cart and passed it to me so I could dump the plate of scones into it.

Grabbing a single one back out, I took a big bite, and my eyes practically rolled back at how delicious it was. Lawrence was one of the few people I didn't have to pretend to be ladylike and proper with all the time, and he smiled knowingly at me. "Thank you," I said through a mouthful of scone, my shoulders bouncing on a laugh.

I had not given Avery a time to meet, considering I was never sure how long these meetings would take. They always seemed to go on for so much longer than necessary. Lords and other noblemen went on and on about gods knew what, while I usually stayed quiet and observed. I probably should speak up more, but they just liked to talk about themselves, what they believed they could do for the kingdom, and why they should be rewarded. But it was always just *talking* and nothing more.

I rolled my eyes at the thought of Chaz showing up late for the meeting and then having the nerve to glare at me for the remainder of it.

As I made my way toward the stables, I attempted to be as discreet as possible. I did not want anyone to see me in case they had already seen Avery on her way there. I knew this was risky, but we needed to understand how to use our powers, and we needed as much practice as we could get in order to make them stronger.

Quiet laughs sounded from inside the stables. I peered around the opening to find Avery and Xander playing around with the practice swords. I hated having to ruin whatever moment they might have been having, but we needed to do this.

I cleared my throat to get their attention. They immediately stopped what they were doing and turned my way.

I held the basket up in offering, "I brought scones."

"Oh, thank *god.* I'm starving!" Avery practically cheered as she ran over to take the basket from my hands.

She offered one to Xander before stuffing one in her mouth, and he held back a laugh before accepting it from her hand.

"I'll see you later," Xander said to Avery before making his way toward the exit.

Before he made it out, footsteps echoed from outside. Panic rose inside me as my eyes darted from Avery to the doorway. Avery looked like she had frozen in fear, so I took it upon myself to hide. As Xander ran for the door, I dove for the nearest haystack, the hay flying into the air around me and sticking to my hair and clothes, but it did little to cover me.

Ben walked in, looking from Avery to me, his eyes wide and forehead creased.

"Wh-what!?" He shouted, pointing a finger back and forth between Avery and me.

"Should I knock him out?" Xander offered, pointing at Benjamin with his thumb. "Maybe he'll wake up and think this was just a dream."

Ben took a step back, his mouth opened like he was going to scream, and Xander dove for him. He did not do anything other than cover his mouth with his hand and murmur for him to shut up.

Avery's head shook like she was finally just realizing what had happened. She really needed to work on her reaction time.

"Don't hurt him!" She told Xander, and he shrugged like he was still considering it. We all knew it was bullshit. He had his chance, and all he did was cover his mouth to quiet him.

"I won't hurt him if he shuts up." Xander gave him a pointed look. Ben nodded, though his eyes were still wild as they darted between us all.

Xander looked to Avery before slowly removing his hand from Ben's mouth. Ben looked like he wanted to scream again, but to his credit, he did not.

Avery gently made her way toward them as if he was a skittish cat, arms raised like she was afraid she'd spook him.

"I don't understand," Ben said, his brows pinched together like he was trying to piece it all together.

I rolled my eyes in exasperation. There was no point in denying it now. We just had to hope that we could trust him. "Clearly, there are two of us. One of us," I gestured to Avery. "Was hidden away shortly after we were born. No one can know about this." I raised my chin as I stared him down. "*No one.*"

Ben bent down on one knee, raising his hand to his heart. "I swear to all the gods, the sun, the moon, and all the stars in the sky, I will do whatever I can to protect you both."

I eyed him for a moment before nodding my approval, and he rose to his feet once again.

"So, only one of you knows how to fight, and that is why the other was terrible today?" Ben's mouth snapped shut as recognition of what he had just said dawned on him.

"Hey!" Avery folded her arms across her chest as she pouted at his assessment, causing Ben's cheeks to immediately flush with embarrassment.

"I am so sorry, Princess. I did not mean... I just... well...." he trailed off anxiously.

Xander chuckled lightly, though he tried to hide it behind his hand, it was too late, and I let a giggle escape me as well.

"What is it?" Ben and Avery asked in unison.

"She really was terrible," Xander didn't try to hide his laughter this time.

Avery elbowed him in the side as she glared up at him. "That's just rude." She turned her back to him to face Ben. "So, we don't have to worry about you telling anyone anything?"

"My duty has always been to the throne and to the Princess of Soluna... however many of you there might be...." he cleared his throat. "I will say nothing."

"Perfect!" I said excitedly as I clapped my hands together once. "Ben, you guard that entrance, and Xander, you guard the other side."

Ben did not waste a moment before doing exactly as I had ordered. Xander, on the other hand, glowered at me.

"Since when do I take orders from you?"

"Please?" Avery cut in with a sweet smile, and Xander rolled his eyes and stalked off the way I directed him to go.

Avery and I looked at one another as we prepared to practice. We closed the distance between us and stood directly in front of one another. She raised her hand for me to take, and I noticed she was shaking.

"Are you okay?" I whispered.

"Yes, just nervous." She shrugged a shoulder.

"It will be alright," I promised, even though I knew I couldn't promise that.

A wave of dizziness struck me as I reached up to take Avery's hand. My entire body began to weaken, and I struggled to stand. Avery caught me, and I instantly felt better when her hands touched my arms.

"What happened?"

"I don't know. I just felt... weak." My mind instantly went back to when I poured my power into the barrier around the castle and realized it must be draining me. "My power is draining. I think the longer I have this barrier up, the more it will affect me."

"Well, let's see what we can do. Maybe I can help with the barrier, so it's not so exhausting for you," she offered.

I stood up straight. When Avery offered her hands this time, I took them without any issues. Avery closed her eyes, a crease forming between her brows in concentration, and I did the same.

"What should we think about?" She asked.

"Just focus on the power inside you and what it can do."

Rain hounded outside. Despite the weather we had earlier, it was a clear night up until this point. My eyes shot open, and I glanced outside to see the rainstorm that continued to pour. Avery jerked back but did not pull her hands from mine.

"I think I did this earlier today. It was cloudy, so I didn't think much of it, but I was daydreaming about the rain and how I used to dance around in it with my mom, and then it started to fall just like I envisioned."

"That is great! Have you had any luck with your telepathy?" I questioned, and her gaze dropped to the ground guiltily.

"I haven't tried. I've been too scared. I don't know why."

"It's okay." I offered her an encouraging smile. "I think you should try, though. It could help us figure out who we can and cannot trust here."

"That makes sense." She pulled her hands back and bit at her nails nervously.

"Try it on me. This way, we can know if it is working or not." I was not sure why we did not think of it sooner. "Let's start with something easy. What number am I thinking of?"

She studied me for a second before answering, "Two," she guessed.

"Yes!" I hoped it would work but was still pleasantly surprised that it had. "Again," I said.

"Eight," she guessed again.

"Yes!" I almost jumped in glee. I was so happy that we finally had a plan that might help us. Okay, so it was not exactly a plan, but it was something.

"Okay, this time, I am thinking of a colour." I quirked a brow.

"Orange."

"That's right!" This time Avery jumped with joy, and I did not try to stop myself as I joined in. "We can definitely use this to our advantage."

Heat flared inside me due to my excitement, and the stack of hay next to me suddenly burst into flames. Avery and I both stopped our girly jumping and stared, open-mouthed, at the fire that came to life beside us.

"I-I think I did that," I said, not even looking at Avery, my eyes fixed on the fire. An idea hit me, then. "Try to put it out with water." I grabbed her wrist, spinning her toward me as I jerked my head toward the fire.

"But what if I start making it rain inside here by mistake?" She recoiled.

"That is why we are practicing. We did not even know we could do this. What better way to practice?"

"Okay," she nodded once and then closed her eyes as she focused again. Her entire face crinkled as she concentrated.

A second later, the flames were *technically* gone. Just not the way she imagined.

Avery opened her eyes to find that the flames were now covered in ice. They looked completely solid as if someone had crafted an ice sculpture to look like flames.

"At least you didn't make it rain inside the stables," I offered with a snort of a laugh.

She blinked several times in shock before finally cracking a smile. "It's a start."

CHAPTER NINTEEN

Avery

Even though we had spent almost every waking hour of the last few days working on discovering exactly what our powers could do, they still had me continue my physical training with Ben. I didn't enjoy it in the least, but I knew I needed to be stronger if I wanted to be ready for when and if those things attacked again.

Ben's knowledge about the two of us definitely made things tremendously easier. We still had to be careful not to be seen around the castle simultaneously but having someone who could help sneak us around or cover for us was helpful.

As I laid in bed, I groaned as the aches all over my body flared to life again. I was hiding out in my room, praying they would give me a break from the constant training.

"You're stronger together," whispered the voice I'd come to recognize as Calypso's.

The room was empty. I searched for her around the open space and came up short, which meant I was either hearing things or she was somehow speaking to me telepathically. I never could have fathomed that I'd consider telepathic communication to be the more plausible scenario.

Calypso was *always* cryptic with whatever she said, like everything was a riddle that we needed to figure out for ourselves. For once, I was glad that I actually understood what she was telling me. It was clear that Amara and I were stronger together. We had more power and magic than we had ever even imagined.

"What else should we be doing?" I asked the empty room, hoping that she could hear me and would respond.

"Work together, become stronger. Together your light will shine brighter."

"What else can we do?" I demanded.

"You will need your light to defeat the darkness."

"Well, that's more than I usually get," I sighed. "Can you tell us who is behind this?" I paused, waiting for a response. Of course, that was it. She was gone.

I screamed into my pillow to let out some of my frustration. It was definitely more than Calypso usually offered, but I didn't understand why she couldn't just tell us exactly what she wanted or who was behind this. I always yelled at the T.V. when this shit happened in movies, but it was about a thousand times more infuriating when it happened in real life.

A knock sounded at the door, and I jumped up and considered who it might be. Was it Calypso in the flesh coming to see me and deliver us real answers? Probably not, but a girl could dream.

"Just a moment," I called as I searched around the room for my clothes, which I had thrown on the floor the night before. Amara liked to keep her room nice and tidy at all times. I, on the other hand, did not. I gave up and ran into the closet to quickly change into a clean pair of leggings and a top before heading to the door.

When I opened it, I was greeted by an overly excited Hazel.

"I was hoping you'd be here," she cheered as she pulled me into a tight hug, and a laugh escaped me.

"Here I am."

"I know I saw you the other day, but that didn't count. I had to bring you to my brother. Barf, by the way. How are we supposed to share secrets when yours are about my brother?" She wrinkled her nose in disgust. "So, I figured I would steal you away today to hang out for a bit to make up for it."

"Steal me away to where exactly? We are still under lockdown." I was all for hanging out with Hazel today and skipping on any more training. But I didn't want to risk her trying to sneak us out of the castle again. It wasn't safe.

"Honestly, I don't even care where we go. I just need some girl time." Hazel wasted no time moving further into the room and plopping herself on the bed. "Just, you know, skip all the gross parts if you want to discuss Xander." She winked.

I rolled my eyes as my amusement lifted my lips. "You're insane."

"In the best way," she said, and I couldn't help but agree.

"I have to admit, I don't get a lot of girl time, so I don't exactly have any suggestions." I shrugged before falling into the chair near my dresser.

"Well, we can't sneak out of the castle. But we *can* sneak into the kitchens and steal the best snacks!"

"Snacks, you say?" I raised a brow and shot her the best mischievous grin I could. I loved the sound of this idea already. I was starving and could definitely use some waffles with chocolate sauce and whipped cream. Maybe even some strawberries to top it off. I had no clue if I'd find any of that, but my mouth was watering at the idea.

Hazel shot up, grabbing me by the wrist and pulling me out of my seat and out the door.

"Gentlemen," she nodded at the guards as she tugged me along. They just looked at each other, unsure of what to do.

"See you later," I called, already halfway down the hallway.

We laughed like schoolgirls as we ran around the corridors. I doubted anyone would stop us from just going in and telling the kitchen staff what we wanted and having them make it for us, but sneaking around was way more fun. We slowed as we drew closer, creeping around the corners to ensure no one was there before tiptoeing by.

We made it to the kitchen door, and it swung open just before we were about to walk through it. A woman ran out screaming and crying, her body knocking into mine as she did. I fell on my ass with a grunt. *"Owww,"* I moaned, and Hazel lent me a hand to help me up.

"G-guards!" The woman called out through her sobs, and I shared a concerned look with Hazel.

Four guards came running over, one moving to try to console her while the other three marched toward us.

I fixed my attention on the woman. This was the perfect opportunity to try out my gifts again, but her mind was a complete mess of distress and fear. As I watched her speak with the guards, the only thing I could make out was more sobbing. However, it was clear that whatever happened in that room wasn't good.

"What happened?" one of them asked as he turned to me.

"I'm not sure; she just came running out of the kitchens screaming like that," I offered in explanation. I felt a prickle of uncertainty running down my neck as I looked back to the woman, still bawling into the one guard's shoulder.

I took a step toward the kitchen door, but one of the guards halted me. "We should investigate this, Your Highness."

Nodding, I glanced back over to Hazel. Fear flashed in her eyes as we waited for the guard to investigate.

A guard swung the door open, and I tried to sneak a peek at what was inside. He stepped into the kitchens and returned only a moment later, his face pale, eyes wide as his mouth hung open.

"What is it?" I asked.

The other guards all crowded around for the answer.

"Someone has been killed."

My mouth dropped open. "Are... are you sure? Maybe they just slipped and fell and were knocked out?"

He audibly swallowed. "Not with injuries like that."

Several guards walked us back to our rooms. I didn't want to be alone, but I knew Amara would have to make an appearance, so I said I needed to go back first.

Hazel understood and gave me a tight, reassuring hug before she returned to her room, and I made sure to have many guards stationed outside of it. She mentioned she didn't want to be alone either and that she would probably send for Xander and the others to stay with her.

The guards were still outside the room, waiting to escort me to Lawrence, and I had no idea what to do. Once they knew where Amara was, not a soul would be left guarding me. I rubbed my arms as I thought about what the guards had said, and a chill ran down my spine. We were still in a heavy lockdown, which meant no one came in and no one left. So that told me that whoever did this, whoever killed that person, was still inside the castle.

A commotion started outside my door. I lowered my ear to it to try and get a better idea as to what was happening out there.

"I was testing you to see how well my chambers were being guarded. While you all thought I was still in there, I was able to escape. Clearly, you need to do better." Amara's voice boomed from the other side.

I had just barely made it out of the way as she snuck inside, still lecturing the guards on how to properly secure her room until she was slamming the door in their faces.

"You're safe," I cried as I practically lunged at her and pulled her in for a hug.

I was not a hugger, but apparently, I was just hugging everyone lately.

"So are you. I heard that you, well, *I* was there when they found the body. I need to go discuss further lockdown plans, and now we *really* need to figure out who is behind this. I think I am going to have the guards do something about the old servants' passages. They're not exactly secret, but better safe than sorry." A frown pulled at Amara's face before she caught it, hardening it again.

"Okay. Calypso spoke to me again, but I will fill you in on it later."

There was another knock at the door, and Amara and I shared a look before I ran to hide behind it. She opened it and let out a small sigh of relief as she pulled whoever it was inside.

Xander closed the door behind him, his gaze searching for me in the room before finally landing on me.

"Thank the gods," he murmured as he took a large step and wrapped his arms around me.

I really am hugging everyone today, I thought as my arms snaked around him, tugging him in even tighter as I pressed my cheek against his chest.

"I will tell the guards you'll be staying here while I am gone and to keep watch," Amara said, but I didn't pull myself away from Xander's hold. The door opened and clicked shut.

"As much as I would hate to ruin this moment and let you go, I brought you something," Xander said, and I felt the vibrations of his voice as he spoke.

"What? But how did you even know I was here?"

"Hazel told me you were both there when the body was found. She mentioned you obviously had matters to attend to about this and that you were coming back before meeting the Regent in his office. She has Erik and Victoria with her, but

I knew you wouldn't be going and that it would be Amara. I didn't want you to be alone." Xander pulled out of my grip, even though all I wanted to do at that moment was hold him even closer. "She also mentioned that you were on your way to the kitchens to get something to eat, so I stopped to get you something."

Xander held up a bag I somehow missed that was seated next to the door from when he first came in. He started unpacking different foods from the bag, and it reminded me of our picnic the other night. I was struck by the fact that he had come so I wouldn't be alone, and on top of that, he brought food. I was so grateful to him that I couldn't help but throw my arms around him once more.

"Thank you," I said, but my voice was muffled as I buried my face in his chest.

We sat on the floor next to the bed, and it reminded me even more of our picnic date.

"How are you feeling?" Xander asked, gently placing a hand on my shoulder.

"Still pretty shaken. I knew there was a likely possibility that there was someone within the castle walls we couldn't trust, but I didn't expect *this*. And I know it is selfish because I know that Amara and I need to figure out our powers and become stronger, but I am a little relieved to have a day off from all the training, magically and otherwise. Does that make me a horrible person?" I asked, concern tugging at my features. "I didn't want someone to die, and I dread discovering more about this person. Did they have a family? Did they have someone waiting for them to come home, only to be told the worst possible news they could ever hear? They should have been safe here. They—"

"You are *not* a horrible person," Xander cut off my babbling. "You have been going through a lot, and the stress alone could get to anyone. *Of course* you didn't want someone to die." He tried to flash a reassuring smile, but I could tell it was forced. He had family here, people he cared about, and it wasn't safe. He had to have been freaking out as well.

"I'm sorry. I know we are on lockdown, but maybe I can convince Lawrence to let you all go back to Coldoria, where it's safe."

"And leave you here?" he scoffed. "I couldn't do that. I do think it would be good to send the others back, but I am not going anywhere without you," he vowed, and I could see the sureness in his eyes as he held my gaze.

"Thank you," I breathed, closing my eyes in relief.

CHAPTER TWENTY

Amara

Lawrence tried to keep as many people out of the meeting as possible, but everyone was in a panic. The man who had been murdered was a member of the royal guard. Not only did people no longer feel safe here, but one of the people who was supposed to protect *them* had been found dead.

To say his body was mutilated would have been an understatement. His arms and legs were contorted in different directions. His eyes were completely black and soulless, with blood streaking down his cheeks like tears. Black, shadowy veins slithered beneath his skin, like they were still somehow alive inside him, even though *he* was not.

This had to be the work of the Shadow Lord… or Esmeray. Someone here had to be working for them. I did not know how, but I was sure of it. The moment I got close to the body, I felt something wrong from within me. I tried to pour some of my light into him, but it did nothing. He was already gone. I did not know if it would have helped if I had discovered him sooner, before he died, before whoever or whatever did this was gone.

We had decided to send any unnecessary people out of the castle. We still did not know who was directly behind this, but with fewer people in the kingdom, there would be fewer suspects to worry about. I was nervous we would unknowingly send whoever was responsible away, but I was confident that whoever did this was not even close to being finished. I was confident that they were after myself and Avery. We had to figure out who they were before they got to us or anyone else.

"I will compile the list of everyone who will be evacuated within the hour, and we will give them an additional two to pack up and leave. Anyone who needs a place to stay will be welcome at the inn in Estrella until this is sorted. Does anyone have anything else to add? " Lawrence caught my attention again, and I looked around at the few people who sat around the table with us.

They all mumbled their agreements and stood to leave. Lawrence and I stayed behind, sharing a look, which I knew meant we needed to speak in private. We waited for them to exit and followed several feet behind them.

As soon as we stepped inside Lawrence's office, he turned his radio on just like he had before. He turned to me immediately, his eyes wild. "That was dark magic." This was the most emotion I'd ever seen from him. He began pacing in front of me, then stopped and whirled on me. "Do you still have the grimoires I gave you?"

"Yes, I do. But—"

"Are you sure none have gone missing?" He demanded.

"Yes, I am sure."

"We need to destroy them!" He turned to his desk and started plucking book after book from the shelves.

"I do not think that is necessary. I still have them and still have so much to learn. Maybe there is something in there that can help us," I reassured, reaching up and stopping him from pulling out more books.

His eyes were filled with true terror. "That is how I found Liliana's body."

"What?" I gasped, pulled my hand back, and looked at him suspiciously, waiting for him to explain.

"I told you she had been experimenting with dark magic. That is what happened to her. *That* was the ultimate price. What if that guard found one of the books that I gave you and was doing the same thing?"

"And I told you, I still have them all. It's just not possible. I believe that the Shadow Lord or Esmeray, possibly both, are behind this. They must have someone working for them here. We *will* figure this out. You work on compiling your list of who we need to evacuate." I did not waste another second before marching out of the office, determined to solve this mystery.

I spent the last hour going through the books Lawrence gave me. There were a lot of spells that could be considered dark magic there, but I did not find anything that could do *that* to a body. The memory of the way the darkness slithered beneath his skin sent shivers under mine. I was missing a piece of this puzzle and needed to figure it out quickly.

It was clear the best defense against the shadow demons, and probably dark magic, in general was Avery's and my power. We needed to work on strengthening it, and I had the perfect test for us to try and do just that.

Back in my bed chambers, I found Avery and Xander seated on the floor by my bed. They both turned guiltily to me as I stepped inside.

"Hey," I said while raising a hand in greeting.

"Hey," they replied in unison, standing abruptly.

"How did it go? What's the plan?" Avery asked eagerly.

"We are going to evacuate all nonessential people." Her gaze shifted to Xander.

"I'm staying," he insisted, and she nodded like she had already expected it. "But I would like Hazel and the others to leave. We already discussed it. It is a good plan for now."

I was surprised by the compliment, if one could call it that. "Thank you, but it was more of Lawrence's idea than my own," I admitted. "I do think we need to work on our magic. I want to try and strengthen the barrier around the castle after everyone leaves. If we do it together, I think it will be so much stronger."

"Good idea. Calypso told me that we needed to work together to become stronger and that our light would shine brighter that way." Avery chewed on her nails nervously.

"That makes sense. We will wait for everyone to get out safely, and then we will try."

While most of the nobles returned to their homes and holdings, a few remained behind. We kept some of our finest guards at the castle while we deployed the remainder to Estrella. I was convinced that any other attacks would be aimed at the castle as that was where Avery and I both were. I wanted to make sure that we had enough guards stationed both at the castle and throughout Estrella to handle the influx of guests and anything else that may come up.

Chaz was one of the few who had insisted on remaining in the Castle, stating that if we did not send any of the royal guards to Caelia, he would not go either. Caelia had their own guards, and he knew we could not risk sending any of our own. Xander volunteered to keep an even closer eye on Chaz when I informed him and Avery.

I would prefer not to have any more attacks or fatalities, but at least now, if anything did happen, there were so few left of us at the castle. There were fewer targets and fewer suspects now. Moreover, fewer people that could potentially be in harm's way.

As the sun began to set, Avery and I prepared to reinforce the barrier I had cast around the castle's perimeter. I positioned myself at the perimeter in a less populated area of the castle grounds, waiting for Avery to arrive.

It was only a matter of minutes before three distinct pairs of footsteps sounded behind me. Turning, I found Avery, Xander, and Ben approaching. Avery and Ben raised a hand in greeting.

Once they reached me, I leaned in close to Avery. "What is with the backup?" I whispered, jerking my head in Ben and Xander's direction.

"I figured it wouldn't hurt to have it," she shrugged, and I suppose she was right.

"We should be quick; I know there are not many people here, but we don't want to risk anything either." I twisted to face the edge where the invisible barrier stood, holding a hand out in offering as I waited for Avery to accept.

"Yes, ma'am," Avery saluted me, a grin pulling at her mouth, and I rolled my eyes as I tried to hide my own.

Ben and Xander were quiet as they stood a couple feet away and watched intently. I expected Xander to have something to say, but he must have realized the gravity of the situation and remained silent. To be honest, he had been serious about helping me find out who was behind this, so I should not have been shocked.

Avery placed her hand in mine, and the second she did, I felt that same warmth from before inside me. It spread to every inch of my body, and as I looked down, that bright golden glow radiated off me. From the corner of my eyes, I noticed that Avery had a faint silver shine around her like before. She shivered, and as she caught my gaze, her smile beamed.

"Do you feel that?" she asked, and I nodded slightly, returning a soft smile her way.

Shifting my attention back to the barrier before us, I took a deep breath as I tried to let the warmth of the power inside me flow and push toward the existing barrier.

Avery's hand began shaking in mine, and I glanced her way again. Her eyes were closed as she concentrated, her whole face pinched as she tried to push her power out. I gave her hand a reassuring squeeze and returned my focus to our task.

The faint light of Avery's power dimmed in my periphery, and I pushed even more of my power into the barrier to strengthen it.

And then, a sudden, blinding light shot out around us, and everything went dark.

"Wake up! You must keep trying, must keep fighting!" Calypso's voice called out to me in the darkness.

My eyes opened, and I found myself in the infirmary. I was unsure how I ended up there or what exactly happened.

The last thing I remembered was pushing more of my power into the barrier. *The barrier!*

"Did it work?" I shot up, desperately needing to know the answer.

Avery, Lawrence, Ben, and Xander stood around me as I lay on one of the beds. They all exchanged wary glances, refusing to look my way.

"I don't think so," Avery finally answered, biting her nails.

"What? How? I poured everything into it!" I wanted to scream, but still felt too weak to even manage that. It was obvious I gave it everything I had. I struggled to keep myself sitting upright as I sat forward in the bed.

"It's my fault," Avery cried. "I just couldn't do it. I'm so sorry."

A pang of guilt washed over me. "It is fine. We can try again. This is probably what Calypso meant when she told you that you had to work even harder for your light to shine.

It makes sense that you are more closely connected to the moon, and I am more connected to the sun."

"This is my fault; you're here because of me."

"I am fine, just tired. I will be okay. I swear." I crossed my fingers in an X over my heart.

She let out a long sigh of relief, "Did you need me to get you anything?"

"I will get the healer, just to be sure," Lawrence cut in, then headed for the door.

But before he could make it there, a loud crash echoed around us.

CHAPTER TWENTY-ONE

Xander

Ben and I dashed into the corridor, only to find it enveloped in a thick, ominous fog. I flailed in the darkness, trying desperately to figure out what the hell was happening. The shadowy smoke wrapped around me as a stinging ache raced through my body everywhere that it touched. I tried to locate Ben as the darkness consumed everything, but I couldn't spot him.

"Prince Xander!" he shouted, and I turned every which way to try and find him, but it was useless. I was blinded by the haze of shadows.

Reaching around me, I tried to rely on my other senses. "Where are you?" I called out but didn't receive a response.

I managed to back myself up against a wall and held myself there as I tried to come up with an idea. I couldn't take out my sword. I didn't know if there was anything else in this darkness with us, but I couldn't risk stabbing Ben or anyone else.

"I'm up against a wall. What about you, Ben?" I yelled out again. *Did I lose him?* "Ben? Are you still there?"

"I'm here. I'm just— I'm having a hard time breathing."

Fuck. That wasn't good. I could still breathe fine, but maybe it was only a matter of time before I started feeling the same effects.

"We need to get out of here, find the other guards, and get everyone else out too. Maybe if we make it outside, you'll get some fresh air, and hopefully, we'll be able to see again."

A hand grabbed my arm, and I stilled, fighting off the first instinct to attack. "Is that you?" I asked, hoping he could get a few more words out.

"Y-yes," Ben stuttered, his voice so low it was hard to hear him, even knowing he was so close.

I used the wall as a guide, leading us back toward the infirmary. I reached the door and turned the knob but had no luck when I opened it. Everything was still pitch black, and the smoke began to sting my eyes the longer they remained open. I squeezed them shut, relying on my other senses to guide me.

"Avery?" I cried out in alarm. *She has to be okay. They all need to be okay.*

"Xander?" Her voice reached me, and my shoulders sagged in relief at the knowledge that she was okay for now.

"We need to make it outside. Can you find the door?" I tried reaching out with my free arm, hoping to find her, but to no avail.

"Avery! Lawrence! Grab my hands. We need to stay together," Amara's voice rang out.

Curses were shouted, and they kept bumping into various things as they tried to reach me.

"Marco!" Avery called out.

"Who the hell is Marco?" I asked sharply, jealousy flaring inside me despite knowing this was not the time.

"No, it is a game. You're supposed to say *Polo*," she sighed.

"This is hardly the time for games, Miss Avery," Lawrence spoke, and I had to agree.

"We can play whatever games you want, but the Lord Regent is right. Maybe after we get out of this mess," I suggested, still holding my hand out and waiting for one of them to grab hold.

"No! Ugh. You don't get it. It's a game to help us find each other in the dark. I say *Marco*, and you answer *Polo* so we can find each other in the dark with our voices."

Ben sagged against me, and I feared we were running out of time, "We need to hurry. I don't think Ben is going to make it much longer." I clenched my teeth as the burning pain returned and agony seared my flesh. "Marco," I gritted out.

"Polo!" Avery called again.

"Marco."

"Polo!" I could tell by the volume of her voice that she was getting closer.

"You're on my right," I said as her hand slid into mine. "You doing okay, Brent?" I asked Ben, and he mumbled something incoherent under his breath, but at least he was still breathing.

Ben stumbled into me again, and I placed an arm under his shoulder to keep him steady.

CHAPTER TWENTY-TWO

Avery

Xander led the way as we walked in a chain together, keeping our backs to the wall as we used it to guide us. I wasn't sure if he was just winging it or if he knew the castle's layout well.

I tried to use my telepathy to reach out and see if we passed anyone along the way, but it was too hazy, so I gave up. Using my actual voice was much more effective in this situation. A few people answered along the way, but not many. They joined behind us, and we soon made it to a door that led outside.

Relief swept through me as we emerged outside and into the glorious light of the moon, the fresh air seeping into my lungs and making me cough to clear out my throat.

Amara had already slipped away from us, and Ben and Lawrence followed close after as she disappeared into the darkness toward the perimeter wall. We couldn't risk being seen together yet, so I guessed it was a good idea for her to leave. But I knew she was going to attempt to fortify the barrier. She had just used up all her energy, and yet she was going to try it again.

More and more panicked people poured out of the castle. As others gathered around us, I realized that Xander was still holding my hand, neither of us making any attempts to let go. People around us jostled and shifted, and he drew me in even closer.

"Xander! Amara!" someone shouted.

We turned to find Hazel, Erik, and Victoria pushing through the crowds to get to us.

"What are you doing here?" Xander's concerned voice sliced through the noise as he dropped my hand and pulled each of them into an embrace. I hesitated for a moment before wrapping my arms around Hazel. "You shouldn't be here; you should be on your way to Coldoria. It isn't safe."

"We couldn't leave without you," Victoria whispered as her hands slithered back around his neck and drew him in again.

Scoffing, I crossed my arms and waited for him to push her off. I was probably being overly jealous, but considering how he acted sometimes, I didn't care at that moment.

Xander finally withdrew just as people's shouts echoed around us. They were frantic and rushing in all directions at once, some even using physical force to get other people out of the way.

The same shadowy smoke from inside coiled around us. From within the smoke, shadow demons appeared, their dark glowing eyes boring into my soul. Frozen in fear, I completely lost all sense of thought. My body shook as a hand wrapped around my shoulders, and I realized that Xander was shaking me. I squinted at him as his mouth moved, unable to make anything out as white noise and a screeching echo filled my ears. I blinked slowly at him before shaking my head to clear it.

"Snap out of it! Avery!" His shouting was drowned out by the shrieks of everyone around us.

Avery. Not Amara. I shook my head in recognition.

"They're back?" I questioned, already knowing the answer.

He nodded stiffly. "We need to fight."

"Fight? I can't fight! I can't do anything. I'm useless here."

He tipped my chin up to meet his gaze. "You aren't useless. You just need more training."

"Right, and what a perfect time to train." I threw my arms up dramatically as I took in the horrified people around us.

"No time like the present," he smirked briefly before shoving a sword in my hand and unsheathing his other.

Unable to settle my nerves, my hands trembled as I raised the sword Xander gave me. I considered trying my magic instead, but I wasn't sure if I should use it in front of everyone. I wasn't sure I would know where to begin anyway. So far, I had no fire magic like Amara did, but I didn't want to risk having it and accidentally setting this whole area and all the people in it on fire.

The guards huddled around the servants as they fought to protect us, their swords raised as they managed to make physical contact with the shadow demons.

Erik withdrew the two blades from his side. One had been positioned immediately below the other. He threw one of them to Victoria, and she caught it with ease. They readied their weapons for battle while Hazel stood with the servants, assuring them everything would be okay.

Everything happening around me was too much to focus on. I was too distracted. I needed to concentrate on fighting these demons for myself, but the creatures zeroed in on me and were fast approaching.

Raising my sword, my hands still too unsteady, I swung for a demon as it lunged for me. It knocked the sword out of my grip with ease. The blow sent the blade tumbling several feet away from me, and a frightened scream escaped my lips.

"Xander!" I cried. But he was too far away, fighting off two shadow demons of his own.

This is it. My knees gave out, and I dropped to the ground, my arms wrapping around myself as I hoped to find some comfort in a quick death.

The demon loomed above me, letting out a deafening shriek before its head fell to the ground and rolled next to me.

Erik stood before me, panting with his sword raised as he looked down at me, extending a hand in offering. I accepted it, and he helped me to my feet.

"Thank you," I choked out, wiping away the tears from my cheeks.

"Of course," his lips tipped up briefly before he swung around to decapitate another demon approaching from behind. "It helps if you aim for the throat!" He handed me back the sword I'd lost, and I took it with a nod of thanks.

I was useless there. I couldn't fight and couldn't control my powers well enough. Struggling for a moment to come up with a plan or idea that might actually be helpful, it finally came to me. I needed to help Amara. We failed with the barrier last time, but maybe this time, we wouldn't.

Searching for a way out, I found a small window of opportunity. There was only one side I could flee toward to avoid the demons' assaults. I held my head and sword high and raced toward the opening. Demons swarmed around me, and I swung my sword out in front of me. It would probably not be very effective if I were trying to fight them, but I just needed to clear a path for now.

They moved aside, probably a little too easily, but I tried not to think about that. I needed to make it to Amara. If we were successful, I had a feeling all the demons would vanish like she said they did last time.

I made it out and ran toward where I was confident I'd find Amara. I glanced back over my shoulder as I ran, guilt washing over me as I left everyone there to fight the demons. But I was doing this for them. If we could use our magic to build a more fortified barrier, they would all be safe again.

Rounding a corner, I raced to the edge of the grounds. My legs and breaths became heavy, but I continued to push forward, for once thankful for all the conditioning my training had provided. Spotting three figures standing alone in the shadows along the border up ahead of me, I nearly collapsed as I finally reached them. Ben caught me, helping to keep me steady. I bent over, hands on my knees as I fought to catch my breath.

"Avery," they all seemed to say in unison.

"What has happened? Are you alright?" Lawrence asked, looking back the way I'd come for answers.

"Shadow. Demons. Attacking," I wheezed between each word.

"No!" Amara gasped, covering a hand over her mouth as her eyes welled with tears.

"We need to fix the barrier," I explained, and she nodded, extending her hand, and I took it, giving it a confident squeeze.

"This time, we won't fail."

CHAPTER TWENTY-THREE

Xander

Before I knew it, she was gone. I lost sight of her after a while. They had all started swarming around her, and I couldn't get to her in time. My hunt for her made it nearly impossible to focus on the battle, so I had to stop looking for her. I prayed to the gods that she was okay.

One of the demons materialized in front of me, and I slashed my sword across its chest, then swung around to lop off its head. Before even making it to the ground, the demon burst into smoke and ash. Another one formed to take its place. They seemed much easier to kill this time, but there were just so damn many of them.

"Someone, grab some torches!" I commanded, hoping I was loud enough. From every direction came the sound of shrieks and cries, making it difficult to distinguish any other sounds. I shuddered to think about how much worse this would have been if they hadn't evacuated so many people earlier.

Another horde of demons appeared before me. I wasn't sure how much longer we would be able to last. The other guards were doing well, but we were severely outnumbered, with the majority of the royal guard back in Estrella.

I took a defensive stance and lifted my sword, preparing myself.

Suddenly, they vanished. I whirled around, expecting them to reappear out of the thick smoke, but that had cleared as well. As I looked around me, I spotted guards and servants but no shadow demons. Hazel, Erik, and Victoria stood with them, but Avery was nowhere to be seen.

Did they take her?

"Avery!" My voice boomed as I searched all around for her, but I couldn't find her. As soon as they saw me, Hazel and the others raced to join me.

"Where is she?" I demanded, continuing my anxious search for her. "I saw... I saw a swarm of them going for her, and I haven't seen her since." I refused to remain still until I found her.

"They didn't get to her," Erik caught my arm, reassuring me. "I was able to stop them. She ran that way." He pointed in a direction, and I didn't wait before I took off in a sprint.

She was going to help Amara.

I should have known that Avery would have gone off to help her sister, but after what happened last time, there was no way I was going to let her do so without me there. I cast a look over my shoulder and spotted the others following closely behind me.

They can't see them together.

I stopped abruptly, one of them slamming into me.

"Just in case they return, you should all stay here and wait, help out if needed. I will find her and do a sweep of the grounds." Once again, I took off running.

"You shouldn't go alone," Victoria's voice called behind me.

"I'll be fine," I replied, not even bothering to turn around or slow my pace.

When I spotted the four of them, I sprinted faster until I stood before them. As I took in the display before me, my voice came out deep and harsh, "What the hell happened?" Ben was helping to hold Avery up while Lawrence did the same for Amara.

"It took a lot out of us," Avery answered, knowing exactly where my mind went.

My concern flared inside of me. "*Why* would you run off like that? I-I didn't know what happened to you! The last I saw, a swarm of them was after you, and I couldn't get to you!" I boomed, making Avery flinch, and I realized I was probably being too aggressive. I took a deep breath to settle my nerves. "I was so worried, Avery," I breathed.

"I wasn't any help there; I was defenseless. I knew I could actually be useful here, and I was right. It worked." She *was* right, but that didn't take away the ache in my chest that I'd felt when I couldn't find her.

"We are going back inside to check out the castle. We need to determine the extent of the damage." Lawrence announced as he helped steady Amara.

She shook him off and wobbled slightly, but she was able to walk by herself, slowly.

Avery and Ben joined me, and I wrapped my arm around Avery's waist to help her stand. Ben said nothing as he withdrew his arms from her.

"They're gone?" she asked, and I nodded. "Thank god," she mumbled, and her head sagged against my chest.

"Are you alright?" I whispered against her hair.

"I will be."

It only took a few minutes before Avery regained her strength. She pulled away, and I reluctantly let her go.

"Your arms!" she gasped, desperately pulling at the sleeves of my shirt. Dark veins slithered under my skin, just like those of the dead guard. My eyes grew wide as I took them in, turning my arms over as I inspected them. "We need to get you to the infirmary. Hopefully, they can help."

Ben walked in front of us as we re-entered the building. The castle had been ransacked. Everything in several areas of the castle had been either strewn about or destroyed entirely. Guards and servants tended to one another as we made our way through the main corridors and to the infirmary.

We knew Lawrence and Amara would be here somewhere, so we decided to take some of the old servants' passages. Like the main corridors, sconces hung along the stone walls every few feet. The dim lighting made it difficult to see, but it paled in comparison to the dark shadows we had just faced.

Since there were no windows in the tunnels, we took extra precautions around every shadow we passed. Ben and I both had weapons raised, while my other hand instinctively found Avery's. Her grip tightened with every little sound that reached us.

Ben pushed the door to the infirmary open, and we followed in behind him. There were several people already laid out on the beds. The head healer's face was grim as she looked us over, tears shining in her eyes.

Her forehead creased as she took in the marks along my arms — the same marks all the other people in the beds wore. She looked back at them, then back to us, her head shaking slightly.

"None of them made it," she explained.

I stiffened. I knew what that meant. All of them were dead. And I was next.

"What? They can't be," Avery sobbed next to me, a mix of shock and terror on her expression as she took in the reality of the situation.

The healer said nothing, grief flickering through her eyes as she covered their faces with a sheet.

"How long have they been like this? There must be something we can do!" Avery demanded as she turned to the healer.

"This is how they were brought to me." Her gaze landed on me, "You are the only one with those markings who is still alive."

"You have to save him!" Avery had her hands on the healer's shoulders, shaking her as her sobbing became more strangled and piercing.

I raced over and forced myself between them, peeling Avery's hands off the healer. "I'll be fine. We'll figure this out," I assured her.

"Yes." The healer bowed her head. "I will try everything I can. I will research whatever I have to." Her eyes darted uncertainly between us and then to the door.

I nodded my approval, and she left. Ben held the door for her before following her out into the corridor, giving us some privacy.

"I want to go through some of Amara's books she got from Lawrence. She said most of them were about healing magic. There might be something in there to help us. But I don't want to leave you alone." She took me by the hand and led me to the only free bed. "Maybe you should get some rest."

"I'm not tired," I teased, pulling her down next to me as I sat on the bed.

"I want to try and see if my magic can help. Will you let me?" she asked, biting her bottom lip nervously as she looked up at me.

"You can do whatever you want to me," I smirked, and she rolled her eyes.

I laid down, my head resting on her thighs as I allowed her to work her magic. Her brows pinched with concentration as she closed her eyes to focus, causing a faint silver glow to radiate off her entire body. That light seemed to dim more as it moved toward her hands. She gently placed them on my arms, and I sucked in a sharp breath, not expecting the cool sting that her touch sent through my body.

Her jaw clenched as she kept trying to heal me, to no avail.

A knock sounded at the door, and a second later, Ben peeked his head through the cracked opening.

"I'd hate to disturb you," he said.

"And yet, here you are," I muttered, and Avery gave me an unimpressed look before returning her attention to Ben.

"Your sister, Princess Hazel, Lady Victoria, and Sir Erik are waiting to see you."

"And we can hear everything you're saying, so don't keep us waiting!" Hazel shouted from the other side of the door, and I couldn't help but chuckle.

"You should go to Amara," I whispered into Avery's ear so only she could hear. "I won't be alone now, and I'll see you soon, I promise."

"I'll be holding you to that," she nodded, her smile not quite reaching her eyes as she reluctantly pulled herself away and headed for the door.

"Brent, I actually would like to speak with you alone for a moment first," I called out, and Avery turned back, giving me a questioning look, but I just shrugged at her, and she left.

Ben stepped inside, closing the door behind him. He walked straight up to me, probably realizing that we had to speak quietly if this was to remain between the two of us. I had no doubts that the rest of them had their ears pressed to the door outside.

"Yes, Prince Xander." Ben bowed.

"You like her, don't you?"

He jerked back in surprise. "Who?" Ben asked carefully.

"Avery," I barely breathed the name. It was definitely not something I wanted the others to overhear.

"I do… but not like that. She is a good friend to me," he smiled softly, and I actually believed him.

"Good, because there is something I need you to do for me."

"Anything, Your Highness."

"The survival rate of these markings doesn't look good," I paused, looking around at the bodies and taking in the severity of the situation. "I want you to promise me you will protect her if I'm not around. And even if I am around."

"It is quite literally my job. But even if it wasn't, I would. You have my word," he promised, and I nodded.

"Oh, my gods, *enough,*" Hazel announced as she pushed her way through the door. Erik and Vicky tumbled in after her, and I was confident they really did have their ears to the door then. "What is with all this secrecy? If you wanted some privacy with Amara, that I would get, but why *Ben?*" Hazel asked before shooting a wink his way, and he blushed.

"We have news from your father," Erik interrupted.

My heart sank into my chest, knowing it wouldn't be good.

"He wanted us, and by us, I mean *you,* to go back to Coldoria after what happened. When the guards we sent to bring Stark back showed up alone, he sent word. He demands you return, and he'll be even more furious when he finds out what happened here tonight."

"Fuck what he thinks," I muttered before realizing I should not have said that in front of Ben, but it couldn't be helped. "I will write him back. Maybe I can convince him to send some of our royal guards here to help. We are supposed to be allied, are we not?"

They all mumbled their agreement, but they knew all too well what my father was like and how unlikely it was that he would send help.

But I needed to try.

CHAPTER TWENTY-FOUR

Amara

There weren't many people left in the castle who could be possible culprits, and I was starting to believe Xander's theory that Chaz was responsible. He had the motive and the most to gain from getting rid of Avery and me. He was rummaging through my things, and there was no way to tell just how long he had been sneaking around the castle and snooping through my belongings. He could have discovered Avery a long time ago. That was how *I* discovered her, after all.

My suspicions were squarely on him, so I decided to share the news with Lawrence and have the Duke locked up in the dungeons under supervision.

I had gone through some of the books Lawrence had given me and had tried out several of the spells, but they had not worked, and I was unable to find anything useful.

I flipped another page, unsure which spells Lawrence considered *dark magic*. Nothing I had come across seemed wicked or evil. I did not know what exactly I was expecting. Maybe spells about raising the dead, talking to the dead, summoning demons. None of that was in the books I had read. Then again, there were still many more books to go through.

"I need your help," Wesley's voice called to me, and I whipped my head around to find Avery barging through the door.

Rubbing my eyes, I looked around, hoping to see him even though I knew I wouldn't.

"Pardon?" I asked Avery as my heart sank into my stomach. I knew I had imagined it, but it was still so unsettling knowing that he *did* need me.

"I need your help," Avery said again. "I want to borrow some of the grimoires Lawrence gave you. We need to figure out a way to save Xander, and you said that they were mostly about healing so far. Right?"

Avery ran and kneeled next to my stack of books on the floor beside my vanity desk. I had already gone through the ones in that pile, but Avery started thumbing through the pages and adding several to her own little pile.

"What is wrong with Xander?"

She refused to look at me directly, but I saw her wipe a tear from her face. "He has the same marks beneath his skin as the fallen guard. Everyone who was brought to the infirmary had them. No one else who had them has survived."

"You will not find anything in those books that can help him. I have already been looking for mention of anything like that since we found the guard. I can give you some of the books I have yet to read. If we are both looking, perhaps we can find something faster."

Getting off the bed, I grabbed four books and brought them over to her. She accepted them with a word of thanks and then walked to the bed's other side to plop down and begin reading. I joined her on my side and picked up where I had left off with mine.

After several hours of reading, exhaustion crept in, and we eventually passed out.

He was rotting away in a dungeon calling for me, but I never returned in time to save him. Demons swarmed around him, thriving off his pain. His eyes met mine as he cried out, "Amara!"

Then, the demons were gone, and it was just the two of us as I somehow found myself next to him inside the dungeon.

"I love you," I admitted through a choked sob. "I have always loved you." Tears streaked down my face. I reached up to cup his cheek, but before I could feel the warmth of his skin, he vanished.

A cloud of smoke whirled around the spot where he had been sitting, wrapping itself around my arm and enveloping me in darkness. A pair of fiery red eyes peered out of the shadows and locked onto mine.

"Amara," Wesley's voice taunted from where the eyes unblinkingly watched me.

He stepped toward me, and I caught sight of the twisted smile he wore before pushing me further into the darkness of the shadows.

It was different. This time, Wesley did not push me to save me.

He pushed me to hurt me.

Screaming, I sprang up out of my bed, and I noticed that Avery had as well. Her breathing was heavy, and her face was pale. Her panicking eyes darted around the room, searching for something or someone.

When I first felt the raindrops, I was worried that there was a leak in the ceiling. Avery was doing this. Her water magic must have reacted to the nightmare she was having. I sent a silent prayer of gratitude to the gods that she had not been the one gifted with fire magic.

"Nightmare?" I asked, and she nodded, finally seeming to realize that was all it was. A nightmare. "Me too," I added quietly, taking a step toward her with my arms raised as I tried to calm her enough to stop the downpour she was creating.

As I placed my hands on her shoulders, her breathing slowed, and so did the rain around us.

"It wasn't real?" She hesitated, glancing around at the room once more.

"It wasn't real," I confirmed.

Sharing a common nightmare meant there was more going on than met the eye, but I was certain it was simply a nightmare this time. However, I knew she could not have had the same one this time, not about Wesley. There was something wrong with him in it, and I had refused to believe it was really happening.

"It felt real," she shuddered. The rain finally stopped as she took a deep breath, and I wondered how we would explain this mess. Shrugging it off, I decided that we had more important things to worry about.

"What happened?"

"Demons were attacking again. There was so much death. Everyone around me was dying, and I couldn't do anything to stop them. I was useless and powerless. The Shadow Lord appeared, and then I woke up." Her eyes darted around the room again, and I squeezed her shoulders reassuringly.

"You are here. You are safe. And we *are* going to figure this out. I think Chaz is behind this. I do not know who else it could be within the castle." I ushered her in the direction of the bathroom. "You go take a shower to warm up, and then we can go find Lawrence."

Her feet planted as she hesitated for a moment. "I want to go see Xander. I didn't mean to fall asleep. I want to make sure he's okay," she choked out the past part.

"Go warm yourself up, and then you can check on Xander while I talk to Lawrence."

She nodded once, then headed for the bathroom. The shower started a few minutes later, and I returned to the bed to read while I waited.

"Amara!" Avery screamed in my face as she shook me.

"Wh-what happened?" My eyes met her frantic stare.

"What? You don't remember?" she demanded. "I was going to ask you the same thing!"

"You were about to get in the shower, and I sat down to read." I gestured to the books sprawled out around me.

"That was over twenty minutes ago. I came out, and you were sitting there, your eyes glossed over with blood trickling out of them. The same dark veiny markings slithered under your skin. I couldn't get your attention. I tried everything."

"What?" I glanced at the clock on the side table next to the bed. She was right.

Inspecting my arms, I did not see any markings. I reached up and brushed my fingers just under my eyes, but it was dry. No blood, no anything.

"You must have just imagined it?" I assured her, but I was not so sure myself.

"I know what I saw," she scoffed, scowling down at me.

"We have seen a lot of things we cannot explain lately. Some real, some illusions." She had been right, though. I knew it was not long, but I had still lost track of that time. It felt like seconds to me when in reality, it was minutes. "You should go check on Xander. I'm fine."

"Right," she rolled her eyes while she grabbed the books I had given her and put them in her satchel. "Don't do whatever it is you just did again," she said as she made it to the door.

"I will try." I was not even sure what I did, so I wasn't sure how I could possibly promise that.

She tossed me a pained smile and then left.

Taking in a deep breath, I rubbed my temples and stood. I needed to talk to Lawrence and ensure that Chaz was locked up.

Since Avery had left through the main door to my room, I figured it best to use the old servants' passages. I had added extra locks so that no one could enter my bed chambers through that way unless they had the key that only I had. Not even Avery had access to it.

In the tunnels, there was nothing but darkness, the echoes of my footsteps the only sounds. As I walked, I could not shake the feeling that someone was watching me. My hand hovered over the hilt of the dagger I had strapped to my thigh, fingers twitching as I waited for some unknown threat to reveal itself.

Suddenly, several pairs of glowing red eyes blinked at me in the distance. I forgot about my dagger and called on the power of my light inside of me. The area around me immediately lit up with my golden glow, but nothing was there. Not even the ashes of the demons I had just seen.

Had I really seen them?

Continuing along my path, I kept pushing out my light to guide the way. I did not know why I hadn't thought of doing so sooner.

A scuff sounded further down the tunnel when I reached the door I needed to exit through. I whirled around, casting my light in that direction. A hooded figure shrouded in shadows caught my attention. They took off running down the passageway, and I immediately ran after them.

They rounded a corner, and as I rounded the same corner to follow closely after them, they had vanished from view. It was a dead end.

Where could they have gone? Had I just imagined that as well?

I returned to where I had first seen them, but there was no sign of anything. Slowly pushing the door open, I peered out to ensure it was safe and that Avery was not around. I was confident she was in the infirmary with Xander at that point, but I could never be too careful.

After knocking on Lawrence's door twice, I was about to give up and hunt for him elsewhere. But before I could leave, he finally opened the door, peeking his head out to survey the area before holding the door wide for me to enter.

I took the seat opposite his on the other side of his desk. He played his music to drown out the sound of our conversation and took a cup of tea from the coffee cart stationed on the far side of his office.

Lawrence's hands trembled as he came to join me. He seemed nervous. His shoulders slumped forward as he sat, his mouth opening and closing a few times as if he didn't know how to say what he had to say.

What is going on?

"I saw my sister," he finally said with uncertainty shining in his eyes.

"What? I thought you said—"

"That she died? She did, but I do not know how to explain it. I keep seeing her and other things I should not be seeing."

"So do we," I admitted. "First, it was a dream or a nightmare. But on the way here, I thought I saw more demons and the Shadow Lord. I don't know what's happening anymore. But I believe Xander was right that Chaz is the one behind it. I don't know who else it could be. We should lock him up for now. *We have to.*" I slammed my hands down on the desk angrily. At myself more than anything. I should have just listened to Xander sooner. Maybe we could have saved some lives.

"I am not so sure, but you are correct. We do not have any other suspects, and if it could help save even one life, we need to lock him up. I will inform the guards."

"Thank you," I breathed, wanting this all to be over so I could go back for Wesley.

I needed him with me.

CHAPTER TWENTY-FIVE

Avery

Hazel and the others were in the infirmary with Xander when I entered. They looked at me when I stepped through the door, and silence fell around the room.

Had they been talking about me?

I cleared my throat. "Hello," I said through a shy smile, raising an arm to wave.

"We were just talking about you," Hazel giggled while Xander elbowed her in the ribs from where they sat next to one another on the hospital bed.

"All good things, I hope." Although I shrugged it off, the idea of them gathering around Xander in bed and talking about me made me tense.

"Of course," Xander grinned, his gaze met mine from across the room, and my stomach fluttered with a different kind of nerves now. A small part of me was pleased to see

Victoria roll her eyes at his words. "Could you all give us a moment?"

They all grumbled their annoyances but made no actual objections as they made their way toward the door. As Hazel walked past me, she shot a wink my way, and I fought off the smile that pulled at my lips as I waited for them to shut the door behind them.

"I got some books from—" I started, but Xander raised a finger to his lips to cut me off. I lifted a questioning brow at him in response, and he gestured for me to come closer.

After taking a few steps toward him, I halted. Slowly, he shook his head. I continued forward, my eyes never leaving his as I did.

It wasn't until I stopped inches from him that he stopped shaking his head. His head tilted slightly, keeping our gaze locked on one another from where he sat on the edge of the bed. His hands slid around my waist, pulling me in even closer, and my breath hitched.

"What were you saying?" he asked as he smirked up at me.

"I was saying—" He cut me off again, this time his finger pressing gently against my lips as his eyes cut to the door.

"I would not be surprised if they had their ears pressed right up against the door listening," he whispered.

I lowered my voice. "I got some books from Amara," I glanced at the door as I breathed my sister's name. "I don't know if they can help, but I want to try."

"Thank you," Xander smiled softly as he tucked a stray piece of hair behind my ear. "You know, this is where we had our first kiss." His eyes shifted to my lips and back to my eyes.

"Oh, was it?" I teased, biting my lip and pulling his attention back to them.

"Pretty sure." He shrugged a shoulder and laughed.

Hushed sounds and murmurs came from the other side of the door, and I couldn't help but snort a laugh as Hazel's voice very loudly whisper-yelled, "Shhh! I can't hear!"

"I told you." Xander stood abruptly, and I stumbled, taking a step back as he made his way to the door and tugged it open. "Can I help you?" he asked the others as they practically fell inside the room.

"I knew you were being too loud," Hazel huffed at Victoria and Erik.

"Actually, you were the only one I heard," Xander corrected her. She folded her arms across her chest as she refused anyone's help from where she sat on the floor from her fall.

"I am going to go to the library to try and find something that can help you," I told Xander as I made my way to the exit.

"Why don't we all go?" Erik offered.

"Yeah! We all want you to get better after all." Victoria pulled Xander by the hand.

"Are you even allowed to come?" I turned back to Xander. I assumed he had to remain there until we figured this out, but I guessed I was wrong.

"They have no idea how to help me, and I seem fine for now." He offered us a reassuring smile, but the "for now" was the only thing we all took from it.

"Right, well, the more of us looking for a way to help, the better." I let out a harsh breath and straightened.

We had all found our places around a large table inside the library. I had already gone through the entirety of one of Amara's books and found nothing useful. The others all grabbed books on healing and medicinal herbs from the library to read, but sadly, they were just as useless.

Whatever it was, I knew it wouldn't be found in any ordinary book. It was related to magic or a curse, and as far as I knew, any records or mentions of magic existing within Caelestia had been erased. Everything except the books Lawrence had given Amara anyways.

"This is boring," Erik sighed dramatically, flipping a page for emphasis.

"It isn't supposed to be fun; we're trying to save Xander," Victoria kicked Erik from under the table, and he flinched back. I had to agree with her on that one.

"I want to save him too, but there isn't anything we can do here, and he would probably rather be having a good time than reading some dusty old books." He rubbed at his knee, which I was willing to bet would be bruised soon enough.

"He's right," Xander said, surprising us all as we stopped what we were doing and looked at him. "If these are my last hours, days, whatever, I want to have fun."

"I didn't mean it like—" Erik started, but Xander cut in again.

"I know. But you're right. So, let's do something fun. Maybe we can still do some research while also having fun?" he offered.

"I could go grab us some booze, but I don't know how to turn *this* into *fun*." Erik didn't wait for a reply before flying out of the library.

I tried to ignore them as best I could. Their books wouldn't hold any answers, but mine might. I didn't need fun; I needed to save Xander.

Erik ran back into the library surprisingly quickly, carrying a few different bottles. He placed them in the centre of the table with a mischievous grin.

"Let's just take a short break from the books and play a game." His eyes practically twinkled with the idea, and I pretended not to hear him as I turned the page of the book I was reading.

Xander placed his hand on the book to stop me. When I raised my chin to meet his gaze, the corner of his mouth tilted up. "A break doesn't sound too bad, does it?"

"It does if it takes time out of trying to help you," I huffed.

He leaned forward, whispering in my ear. "It will be fun."

"Fine," I grumbled, closing my book.

"Yes! What should we play?" Hazel practically cheered, reaching for a bottle and taking a swig.

"You couldn't bring any glasses?" Victoria asked as she gave him a pointed look. Though I don't think it bothered her too much since she took the bottle from Hazel and followed her lead.

Erik only shrugged as he grabbed another bottle from the middle of the table. "*Never Have I Ever* could be fun," he suggested, and everyone mumbled their agreement.

"I'll start then." I had never played the game, but it was pretty straightforward, and I knew enough about it from movies. "Never have I ever played this game." I looked at them with a smug smile, confident I had won that round. And just as I expected, they all took a drink.

Then it hit me. I may not have been able to keep reading to find a cure at that moment, but it was the perfect opportunity to practice my telepathy. And if it helped me have an advantage in this game, then that was even better. I'd never considered myself competitive, but I wanted to win this. I didn't even know if you could technically win at this sort of game, but I guessed whoever was the soberest by the end *would.* Since I didn't partake in much before coming here, I was confident that that would definitely be me.

They all took another drink, and I realized I'd missed whatever Victoria had just said for her turn. *Oh well.*

"Never have I ever been arranged to be married," Erik fought to hold in his laughter as he looked between Xander, Hazel, and me.

"Oh, so we're just targeting people now, are we? Okay, this just got even more interesting." Xander took a drink, and I couldn't help but watch his throat bob as he drank. It took me a second to realize I had to drink to that one.

Thanks, Amara.

"Never have I ever kissed more than one person in twenty-four hours," Xander said as he tipped his bottle to Erik with a smug smile on his lips. I expected him to drink then, but he didn't. Hazel and Erik were the only ones to drink for that one.

"Never have I ever sung karaoke." Hazel pressed her lips tightly together as she suppressed a laugh. She didn't drink, but the rest did.

"What? I thought you loved karaoke?" I asked her, my brows crinkling with confusion.

"Oh, gods no. I just love making other people sing it," she admitted, and I cast her a light-hearted glare.

"That's evil!"

She shrugged a shoulder as she exploded into laughter.

I fixed my attention on Erik as his eyes squinted, and he looked like he was internally debating something.

"No...shit, I've done that too. Pretend to be sick? Nope, done that. Been black-out drunk? Done that many times."

"Never have I ever been black-out drunk," I smirked, and Erik cocked his head slightly. I realized I probably shouldn't be so obvious about stealing something the second they think it, but I did need the practice.

We played a few more rounds, and I was slightly less obvious about taking people's suggestions from their heads. I'd wait for a few rounds to use it, which worked better, especially since everyone else was drunk by that point. Xander and I were the only semi-sober ones left by the time the others decided they needed food and left us alone in the library.

I reached for the book I was reading earlier from the side of the table where I had pushed it earlier, but Xander's hand stopped me yet again.

"Thank you." He was so close I could feel his warm breath against the shell of my ear as he spoke.

"Of course." I tilted my chin toward him.

He held my gaze for several seconds before slipping to my mouth and back. His hand cupped my face as he leaned in closer. His lips brushed against mine so gently I barely felt them. If it weren't for the warmth that the feeling ignited inside me, I would have questioned if it had even happened.

Xander withdrew, and my arms shot out instinctively around the back of his neck. He watched me, waiting for me to say or do something, but I didn't know what I should say.

I'd always pulled away from people and never let them close. Intimacy was always so scary for me. It's not as though Xander was my first kiss or anything like that. But maybe he was my first something; I just didn't know what. All I knew was that I didn't feel the need to pull away with him like I did with others in the past.

Capturing his mouth with mine, I drew him closer again until our bodies pressed flush against each other. The warmth of our bodies battled against the cool kiss of my magic within me, stoking it.

As his fingers knotted in my hair, my magic took over, spilling out of me. I placed my hands on Xander's arms as our kiss deepened, and he shivered under my touch. I was sure the icy touch of my magic had more to do with it than my effect on him, but I couldn't be sure.

I was the one to pull away, and my eyes grew wide as that faint silver glow I was beginning to recognize as my magic shined around his arms where I had touched. The black slithering marks stopped moving and soon faded into silver lines before fading altogether.

Xander looked at me with nothing but awe in his eyes. The marks were gone. I didn't know if they'd stay gone, but all that mattered was that they were gone for now.

"How do you feel?" I asked, inspecting his arms.

"You did it!" Xander kissed me again, but I was too surprised by what I had done to do anything else. He pulled away just as quickly as he had kissed me. "You really did it. Thank you."

"Of course," I muttered. If I could figure out how I actually did it, I could save other people if it happened again. "I just wished I knew how."

"I hope you don't have to kiss everyone to save them." Xander raked his hand through his hair as he chuckled.

"Who knows?" I bumped his shoulder with mine, teasing him. "I'm just glad you're better, though I don't know how to explain that to everyone else."

"Leave it to me." He winked. "I should go check on them, though. Did you want to come with me?"

"I would, but I have to go see Ben. Come find me later, though." I turned and waved a hand in his direction as I headed for the door.

"Always." He grabbed my hand, spinning me around to face him again, before placing another quick peck on my lips and racing to beat me out of the library.

Training with Ben was brutal. The guy did not take it easy on me. In fact, I swear he pushed me even harder, knowing I had no prior sword or hand-to-hand combat training. I was panting on the ground of the stables, trying to catch my breath as he held out my water for me to accept.

I drank half, then poured the rest over my face trying to cool myself off. After I did, I called on the water magic inside of me to refill my bottle, and it did just that. I smiled appreciatively at the water bottle as it was full once again.

"Okay, break time is over. Let's get back to it." He held out his hand and helped me to my feet.

"It's been hours. Why are you pushing me so hard?" I groaned, rubbing at the sore muscles on my arms and legs.

"Why do you want to train at all?" He didn't ask it in a rude or demeaning manner, but like he genuinely wanted to know.

"Because I don't want to feel helpless or defenseless if we were attacked again," I answered without hesitating, surprised by how honest and unashamed I was to admit it.

"That is why I am pushing you so hard. I don't want you to have to feel that way."

Ben threw me an actual sword, not a wooden practice one this time. It was smaller and lighter and, if I had to guess, probably fit for a child, but it was perfect for me. I wasn't skilled in the slightest, but maybe I was slightly better than I had been before, and that was a good enough accomplishment for me.

"That was the first sword I ever received. My father gave it to me when I was younger. I was the youngest of all my brothers. When I was much younger, I read while my older brothers and father trained together. I'd just sit a couple feet away and half-watch, half-read. Eventually, I started training with them, and when I graduated from the training sword, my father gave me this one." He gestured to the sword in my hands.

"I-I can't accept this from you." I stuttered, trying to hand the sword back, but he just shook his head.

"I want you to have it. You were the only person I ever told about my true dream. My father gave me this, thinking it was my dream to join the guard as well. It was not the last one he gave me, even though, of course, there are many memories attached to it. But I want you to have it."

"I don't know what to say. Thank you." I gently placed the sword down and hugged him.

"I think this is enough training for the day. Shall I escort you back to your chambers?"

"Yes, thank you. I should probably wash up before I meet with Amara to practice our magic."

CHAPTER TWENTY-SIX

Amara

"Save me, Amara." Wesley's voice called to me through the darkness.

"Wes, you just need to hang on a little longer. I am coming for you, I promise," I cried, wiping at the tears streaking down my face.

"It's too late," his voice sounded further away now. I was losing him all over again.

"No!" I reached out to find him but found nothing. The darkness consumed him, just like it always did.

Sitting on my bed, my eyes sprung open. Glancing down at my arms, I saw that the black slithering marks were back but soon faded and disappeared altogether. The tears never stopped falling as I looked down at the grimoire in front of me. I had found a spell that would allow me to see someone if the connection to them were strong enough. I used it to see

Wesley. At first, he had been in a dark dungeon, but as soon as I tried to speak with him, the shadows took over.

I didn't even get to really see him, feel him. It was too late; he had said so himself. I had to find him. I couldn't wait any longer, but I didn't know how I could just leave at a time like this. My kingdom and people always had to come first; he knew that. He had pushed me here, yet this didn't feel right. Nothing about this felt right.

The clock beside my bed read nine o'clock, but it could not be correct. If that were the case, that spell would have taken hours, whereas I had only gotten to see Wesley for seconds.

Running to the bathing chamber, the clock there said the same thing. *This couldn't be.* I was supposed to be meeting Avery to practice our magic, though I didn't know what more we had to practice as we seemed to both have a better grasp on things.

Rinsing my face at the vanity, I hoped it would help me clear my head. But my reflection did not look right when I looked in the mirror. My face twisted into a menacing smile, and my hair darkened to a deep brown, almost black colour. The water from the tap continued to run, and I splashed some cool water on my eyes. As I looked back at myself, everything was back to normal.

I made my way to the closet and changed as fast as possible, then hurriedly headed out through the passage doorway. Something about the tunnels seemed off. Not a single sconce was lit. The walls were slick with moisture as I felt my way through the passageways. My heart pounded in my chest with each shaky step I took.

The sound of scuffling footsteps could be heard from farther down the tunnel. I used my light magic to illuminate the area, but I could still only see a handful of feet in front of me. As I moved further down the passageway, my eyes narrowed as movement at the end of where my light reached caught my attention.

A cloak that seemed to be made up of shadows billowed out as the person wearing it sprinted down another passage. Unsure if this was happening or if I was imagining things yet again, I still decided to chase after them. As I rounded the corner they had just taken, they took another and another. It didn't matter how fast I ran. Every time I turned down another passage, they seemed to be heading down a different one.

We headed deeper into the maze of tunnels, and I realized I had never gone this far into them before. As I took one final turn, I noted how the sconces in that particular tunnel were actually lit. Though it was dim, I could easily make out the person who stood with their back to me as they met a dead end.

I have you now.

My hand immediately shot to my dagger strapped to my thigh as I crept up carefully behind them, hoping to catch them off guard.

They turned to face me suddenly, making me jolt back, but I still could not see their face beyond the shadows. I squinted my eyes to get a better look as their hands moved to grip the hem of their hood and lower it.

Shock slammed into my body in recognition as a cruel smirk pulled over their mouth.

"No..." I whispered, all the air leaving my lungs. "It can't be you."

My head pounded, and my hand reached back to rub the spot where a new bump had formed at the back of my skull.

I was inside a dungeon. Wet stones surrounded me. It was hard to tell, but something about the dungeon seemed familiar. Had I seen it in a dream? Was *this* a dream?

A throat cleared, and I whirled my head toward the source. Inside the dungeon, leaning against the cell bars, was Wesley.

Rising to my feet, I could not help but do anything other than stare at him. My mouth parted, but no words came out.

He looked different. His hair had always been a floppy mess, but it was slightly longer. His face needed to be shaven, but the thing that had changed the most was his eyes. They were still a deep blue but looked almost hollow as crinkled lines formed around them.

"You're here," I breathed, finally pointing out the obvious.

Reaching out for him, I was immediately faced with resistance before realizing my hands were in shackles. My brows pinched together as I looked back at him and noticed that he was not.

The chain on my cuffs clanked as I raised my hands and shook them at him. "Help me. We can get out of here together."

He chuckled darkly, "Now, why would I do that when I was the one who brought you here?"

CHAPTER TWENTY-SEVEN

Xander

After practically emptying out the kitchens, we moved the little gathering to my chambers. I wasn't exactly sure where Erik had found more food to hoard and bring with him, but he certainly managed.

It felt like old times as the four of us hung out. Erik and Victoria danced around my room while Hazel and I sat on one of the sofas I had in the little seating area. She cackled as she threw popcorn at them playfully. They had been so relieved when I told them the markings on my arms had vanished, though I couldn't very well tell them that Avery magically healed me when she kissed me.

"Amara must have been happy that those things are gone." She nodded at my arms.

I shrugged, making a face. "Why would she care?"

"Uh… because she was very adamant about finding a way to help you?" Hazel's face scrunched up in confusion as she watched me.

She meant Avery, not Amara. To her, they're the same person.

"Right, yes. She was glad." I cut my gaze back to Erik and Victoria, hoping Hazel would drop the subject, but I knew better than that. It was Hazel, after all.

"Oh, come on. You have to give me *something.* Are you both excited about the engagement now?" Hazel was so loud Erik and Vic stopped what they were doing as they waited for my answer.

I groaned, "I guess."

"You guess?" she balked. "How romantic."

I smirked slightly at that assessment as it reminded me of something Avery, as Amara, said to me one of the first times we were together. Remembering the others were still waiting for me to say something, I shrugged a shoulder again. It was hard enough talking about this in general, but not being able to explain that they were, in fact, two different people made it nearly impossible.

"But you do care for her, don't you?" Hazel questioned as she prodded me with her finger.

"Yes, I do."

"Good, because she is my friend." Hazel kept poking me, and I was tempted to push her off the sofa but refrained.

Erik and Vic continued what they were doing now that I had given them all my answers.

"Look, Hazel, I am sorry if I have not been the best brother lately. The last few years have been especially rough. I miss it when we could just hang out like this. You are not just my sister, but my friend too."

"Why so sentimental all of a sudden?" She arched a brow and crossed her arms.

"You never know when it might be too late to say these kinds of things." I lifted my hands in surrender, and her eyes narrowed.

Finally, she rolled her eyes and accepted my sincerity. "I miss how things used to be, but I guess that happens when you grow up. Besides, I know you did all of this," she gestured around the room, "for me. But I suppose it all worked out in the end for you anyway. Since you *love* her." She elbowed me playfully again.

This time I really did push her off the couch.

"Hey!" she demanded as she stood, hands on her hips, ready to scold me.

There was a knock at the door, and we looked around at one another, wondering who it could be. I got up from the couch to answer it.

One of father's messengers stood on the other side, flanked by four of our guards. I sighed, stretching my hand out for the letter he was clearly here to deliver. Father's letter was short and not so sweet.

> *Prince Alexander II,*
>
> *Return to Coldoria <u>immediately!</u> You have responsibilities here that you are <u>required</u> to attend to.*
>
> *I refuse to send help and am now considering if our allegiance to Soluna is worth this headache. If you do not return with the messenger and guards I have sent to retrieve you, there <u>will be consequences.</u>*
>
> *- King Alexander*

All I wanted the last two years was out of this arranged engagement, and now that I wanted to help Soluna, he was questioning the alliance. How can he compare helping a kingdom we are allied with a headache? Fuck my father and his consequences. They wouldn't be anything I hadn't dealt with before.

I crumbled the letter and handed it back to the messenger. "You can tell him I won't be returning."

"B-But y-your Highness. You...you must," he stuttered, visibly shaking as he refused to meet my eye.

Truth be told, I did feel bad for him. Gods only knew what my father had threatened him and the guards he sent to escort me back to Coldoria with if they didn't return with me. But did I feel bad enough to return? *No.*

The people in Soluna needed us, so the responsibilities back home could wait.

The messenger and guards finally got the hint and left.

"He's not sending help, is he?" Erik asked.

"Of course he isn't. I don't know why I even bothered to ask him," I huffed, throwing my hands in the air.

"Because even though he is cruel, you are not." Hazel squeezed my shoulder reassuringly.

"Thank you," I groaned, still angry with our father.

I didn't want to think about what the consequences would be this time. When I was younger, he would beat me behind closed doors if I disobeyed him. He was also so careful not to leave any marks or bruises where they could be seen. Even so, the rumors circulated.

Once I was old enough to fight back, he devised an even more ruthless punishment: Hazel. He knew she was my only weakness. He never cared about her or paid any attention to her until then. It was all my fault, all because I loved my sister.

"What do you mean, no?" Father scoffed.

If I were younger, I would have flinched. Would have taken it back. But I wasn't going to do that anymore. He knew damn well he couldn't beat me into submission anymore. I

271

wasn't sure how I found the courage, but I managed to smirk at him and raise my chin defiantly.

"Oh? You think you're all grown up, do you? You are not the one in charge here, and it looks like you need some reminding. "Guards, bring her in. This ought to wipe that smirk from your face."

He glared at me. I didn't miss how we were at eye level now, and I no longer had to look up at him.

The guards dragged Hazel in by the arms, her eyes wild and frantic as she looked around at what was happening, and my heart sank. What the hell was he going to do to her?

"Maybe next time, you will listen." Father's face twisted into a mocking grin.

"What are you doing?" I demanded, "Let her go!"

Father just jerked his chin at the guards, two of whom stood at the side of the room, before moving toward me. I tried to fight them off and get to Hazel, but several more came and held me still. The ones who had Hazel marched out of the room, and I cried in horror as worry and fear crept in.

The guards held me back as I struggled to escape their grasp. The ones who had left with Hazel returned rather quickly, and I vowed to get justice at them for whatever they had just done. My father wouldn't be king forever, and you could bet I would remember this.

They handed a key to my father, and I turned to him, hoping he would elaborate on what had just happened.

"She will stay locked up in her room until you learn some respect," was his only reply before turning away from me, motioning for the guards to finally let go of me.

I raced up to Hazel's room, but it was no use. I couldn't open it.

"Hazel, please tell me you're alright. They... they didn't hurt you, did they?" I prayed she was well enough to answer.

"I will be okay. Just a little hungry," she answered through a laugh, but I could tell it was an act, even as the door divided us.

"I'll get you out. I promise."

"I know you will."

Waiting until father passed out, I snuck into his chambers, where he was passed out on a lounger. This was a regular occurrence for him as he liked to drink himself to sleep. Normally I was on the wrong end of his alcoholism, but it suited me just fine for once. Nothing could wake him once he was in this state.

Reaching into his pockets, I soon found exactly what I was looking for. The key.

If I just let her out, Father would know, and it would be obvious what had happened. Now that I knew he would use Hazel to punish me, I had to be smarter. I brought her food, unlocked her door, and sat on the floor with Hazel, holding her so she wouldn't be alone.

After she had fallen asleep, I carried her to her bed. I snuck back into Father's room to deliver the key back and found my way to my own bed for the night.

Father never paid Hazel much attention. I always envied her freedom. She could do anything she wanted and didn't have this pressure I had from him. That all changed that night.

He knew she was my weakness, and he knew how to exploit it.

The ground under our feet began to tremble, and the surrounding walls shook. Around us, debris had started raining down. The air was thick with smoke. Concerned, I glanced around at the group. As dark shadows encircled me, I strained to break free.

A demon appeared from within the shadows, lunging for Hazel. I dove between them, sword raised as I slashed its throat. This one was different from the ones I had seen before. It had the same glowing red eyes and shadows coiling around it, but it was larger, its body not made up of bones and smoke like the others seemed to be. It had horns and wings and some kind of spiked tail. I didn't hesitate to ensure it was really dead. I lopped off its head and stabbed it where I assumed its heart would be.

The shadowy smoke did not leave, but no more demons appeared at that moment. I helped Hazel up from where she had stumbled back on the floor and turned to the others.

"We need to find Avery!" I blurted out without thinking.

"Who?" they all said in unison.

"Fuck. Avery. *She* is the one I—" I paused, clearing my throat. "*She* is the one I care about. It's a lot to explain, but long story short, there are two of them. Avery and Amara are twins, and I need to find them both."

They looked at one another with disbelief in their eyes. But I didn't have time to explain further as roars and screams sounded around us.

"We need to go!" I shouted, and they didn't question me further. We all ran down the corridors in search of Avery.

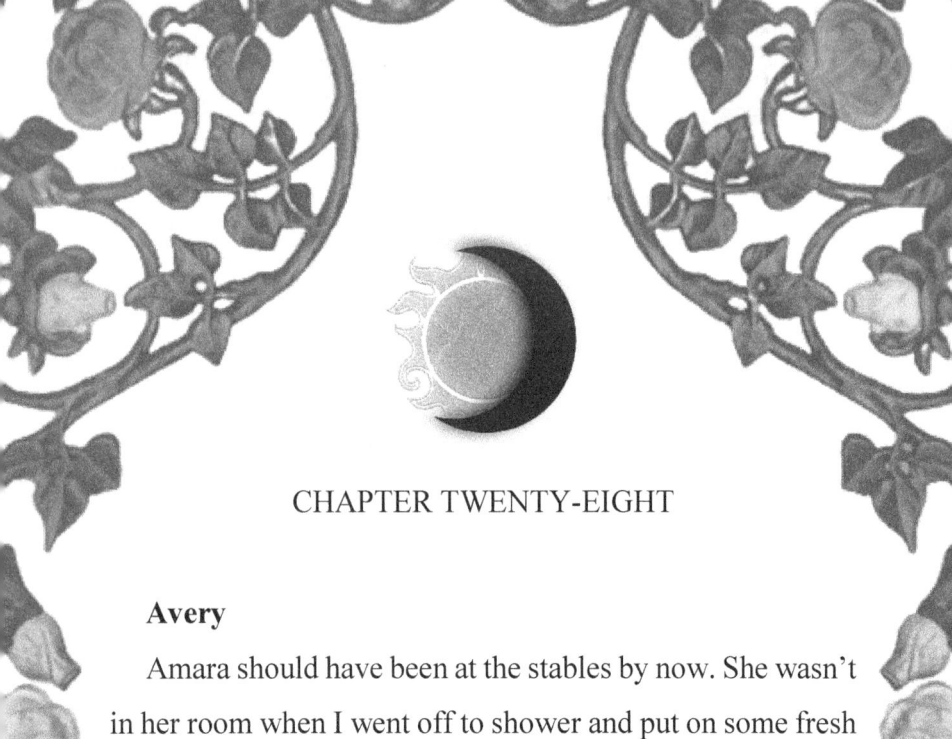

CHAPTER TWENTY-EIGHT

Avery

Amara should have been at the stables by now. She wasn't in her room when I went off to shower and put on some fresh clothes, so I assumed she had left early to meet me, but when I arrived, she wasn't there.

Dark storm clouds filled the sky as thunder and lightning loomed above me. When I looked up, my eyes flashed wide as I noticed that the barrier Amara and I had created was gone. A cloud of thick smoke filled the air, making it almost impossible to see anything more than a few inches in front of me.

I raced out of the stable area toward the castle, and immediately I knew something was wrong. The barrier had fallen, and demons were attacking once again. I gripped the hilt of the sword Ben had gifted me and unsheathed it. I was still horribly uncoordinated, but it was better than nothing.

My water magic was strong, but I doubted it would do well against these creatures as I still struggled with the light inside me. I knew once I could wield it properly, those things would be no match.

A body slammed into mine, knocking me off my feet as my sword skidded away from me. I cursed under my breath as the weight of whoever had crashed into me pressed me into the ground.

I fought with everything I had in me. I kicked, screamed, punched, and flailed, though it wasn't much.

"Ow, Avery," their voice wheezed as I managed to get them off me.

"Ben," I gasped before throwing my arms around him. "Thank god it's you." He reached down and handed me back the sword he had gifted me.

Horrifying screeches echoed around us, but an even more disturbing laugh cut through the shrieks and cries.

Vivian's face appeared before us, the smoke almost parting as she passed through. The smoky shadows seemed to move and dance around her body as a sinister smile twisted her lips.

"Ah, yes. Thank the gods, it's *him.*"

"Y-You? It was you?" I breathed harshly. It was like the air had been taken from my lungs. I stood there frozen in shock, staring at her in disbelief. "I thought maybe it was Chaz, but it was you the entire time."

Ben pushed me behind him as he withdrew one of his short swords and pointed it at her.

"Ha! Chaz? Please. He was nothing more than a pawn, too stupid to come up with real ways to claim the throne. All he needed was a little push." She snapped her fingers, and just like that, Chaz appeared on his knees before her. His arms and legs were bound by the chains made of darkness. More shadows slithered around his face, completely covering his mouth. His eyes were wide as they darted around, then landed on us in a silent plea.

My voice finally returned to me, and I pushed past Ben. "Let him go!"

"If you wish." Her grin was somehow even more menacing than before.

The shadows around his body retreated and made their way back toward Vivian. Chaz's body slumped forward as he was freed, his hands and knees on the ground as he gasped for air. Before he could even attempt to get up, the shadows around Vivian swirled and twisted into a dagger and stabbed him in the back, right through his heart.

Chaz looked at her in shock, then back to me. His eyes were frantic as he wheezed forward once more, blood spilling from his lips before he dropped to the ground. His eyes never left mine, and I screamed in horror.

"Why would you do that? What the fuck is wrong with you?" I cried as Ben attempted to push me behind him once again.

"Why not?" she chuckled coldly. "I didn't need him anymore, and besides, he's not the only one here I have under my control."

All the blood in my face drained as my mind swirled with so many different questions. But before I could voice any of them, her entire body shifted and changed.

She looked like me, but she didn't. Dark, almost black hair billowed past her shoulders as the shadows clung to her, dancing around her body. Her eyes were the same forest green as mine but somehow darker. I recognized her then, from my nightmares.

"Who are you?" Ben shouted as he held his sword raised, ready to strike.

"I think you both already know the answer to that. My real name is Esmeray, and we are one and the same, Avery."

I flinched at her use of my name, my real name. She knew. She knew everything. She was the one behind all of this. She had to be. But how? Why? She was the one that trapped me with the sleeping curse.

"What do you want?" I yelled over Ben's shoulder while he continued to use himself as a shield between us.

"You." She laughed as she pointed her finger at me, and it sent a shiver down my spine.

Ben sprang into action, swinging his blade at her throat. He had gotten within touching distance of her when he abruptly halted.

"Honestly. Have you not stopped to think why your powers don't work on Benjamin?"

"W-What are you talking about?" Ben's arms trembled as he continued to hold his sword mid-air, fighting against what held him.

She rolled her eyes as if he was nothing more than an annoying fly buzzing around her. "Not knowing or willing, but you *did* work for me all the same. Any information you had was all reported back to me before I would wipe the encounter from your mind like it never happened. You've been ever so helpful." She closed the space between them, pushed his sword down with one finger, and then patted his cheek with her other hand.

Tears filled his eyes as he looked from her to me. "No," he croaked. "I would never betray you like that. I would give my life to protect you, I-I— "

"That's enough. I've grown tired of this. Kill her." She flicked a finger in my direction.

"No!" Ben shouted, slowly turning toward me. "I-I can't!" he cried.

"Ben!" I sobbed, frozen in fear.

"Oh, and Avery, don't move." She added as one side of her mouth hooked up into a pure evil smile.

I tried to move then, but my body was stuck in place, and this time it wasn't because I was in shock. It was as if I was paralyzed, unable to even lift my sword that was still clutched in my one hand. Tears fell down my face as Ben jerked toward me.

"You need to run, Avery. I can't control my body!" Ben commanded, but it was useless. I had no more control over my body than he did.

Smoke and shadow curved around him as they influenced his movements. My eyes shot down, and I noticed the same shadows swirling around me, holding me in place.

My gaze shot back to Ben, now only inches away, as he cried and mumbled his objections incoherently.

"It's okay." I held his gaze. This wasn't him. This wasn't his fault. Whatever happened, I didn't want him to blame himself. "You can fight this. You are so strong, and you are the kindest person I know. You can fight this." I smiled softly as more tears spilled.

Ben screamed in pain as he clutched his face with his hands, dropping his short sword. His eyes bore into mine through his fingers as he cried.

"She-she made me. The things she made me do, oh gods Avery, I am so sorry."

Darkness covered everything. Leaving only Ben and me alone as a hurricane of shadows swirled around us, sucking all the light out. Ben continued to move closer as Esmeray's menacing laugh mixed with the whirling wind around us.

"I decided to be kind and gifted him the memories I took away so he can remember everything he did before he kills you."

"Avery, I did it all. I brought you to the dungeons in Coldoria, the terrace, and I brought her your book to curse it. It was all me," Ben choked out between sobs.

"It wasn't you," I assured him, hoping he believed me.

"But it was."

"You were being controlled, Ben. I know you would never intentionally hurt me. Even now, I know this isn't you. Do you hear me? This *isn't* you. We're friends and always will be, no matter what happens. After I'm gone, I want you to remember that I don't blame you, this isn't you, and we're friends."

"We're friends?" he asked as hopelessness filled his eyes.

I fought with all the power I had inside me to move, but the only thing I could manage to do was nod my head once. "We are. No matter what happens."

"Thank you," he said as he stood directly before me.

He yanked the sword he had given me from my hand, raising it high as I closed my eyes and thought of all our happy moments. Of us sharing our dreams, reading and relaxing in the garden, training together, and him gifting me that very sword he held above my head now. Ben had always been such a kind soul, and I hoped he could move past this and forgive himself for what he was going to do.

Warm, thick wetness splashed over my body. *Blood.* I opened my eyes slowly, looking down to where the fatal wound should be, but I couldn't feel it, figuring I had gone numb from the pain. But there was no injury to be found on my body.

That isn't my blood.

My eyes darted to Ben on his knees in front of me, at the hilt of his sword sticking out of his chest, and a sob lodged itself in my throat.

"I told you I would give my life to protect you," he breathed as blood spilled out of his mouth.

"No!" I screamed, still unable to move as his body fell to the ground before me.

Esmeray's laughter rang in my ears as the smoke cleared, and she stood before us once more.

"Well, he was stronger than I gave him credit for; I will give him that. You know what? I'm feeling generous today. Instead of killing you right now, I have decided to let you live a little while longer with the guilt of his death, with the knowledge that this was all your fault, that it should have been you. Besides, I already have one of the doppelgangers." Her grin was cruel as she moved closer. "But don't worry Sweet Avery, we will meet again soon."

And just like that, she had completely vanished, along with the wind and shadows. The storm stopped, and the sun shone almost mockingly in the sky above us, and I realized then that we were in the castle gardens.

I fell to my knees with a whimper and quickly scurried over to Ben's body, pulling him into my arms as I cried. "It's okay, Ben. You're strong. I just have to get you to the infirmary."

"I'm not going to make it. We both know that. I want to die here with you, in your arms, in our favourite spot. I did my job. I saved you." He smiled as his eyes drifted closed.

I screamed for anyone to come and help us as Ben's body went limp in my arms. As tears poured down my cheeks, I pressed a kiss to his forehead, hoping it would save him the same way I had saved Xander. But I knew it was too late.

Ben was gone.

The Story Continues...

The story isn't over yet! Twingenuity Book Three will be out sometime in 2023! For more updates follow me on social media and join my monthly newsletter!

Visit www.daniellehillwrites.ca or follow me @daniellehillwrites on Instagram and Tiktok!

ACKNOWLEDGMENTS

I need to thank all my incredible friends and family who have been there for me and helped support me through this amazing journey. I would especially like to thank Stephanie Bate, Kamarah Dailey, Abigail Woodcock, Rachel Fagan and Sydnee Birkeland for always being there when I needed to run ideas or even full scenes by you your opinions.

Steph, thank you for being such an amazing friend, editor and huge supporter in general!

Rachel, thank you for doing some final edits and looking over everything for me. I loved hearing your thoughts and theories as you read it for the first time.

Syd, thanks for being the best blurb writer/editor especially for a book you hadn't gotten the chance to read yet!

An enormous thank you to the best editor I could have asked for, Emily Anderson. This book would not be what it is without you. You are an amazing editor, and I love how much of a perfectionist you are! What more could you want in an editor anyways? Thank you so much.

Ashley Lavadinho, you're a great editor and even greater friend. Thank you so much for all the work you have put into this book and all future ones to come!

To Celin, you completely blew me away with this cover. It is just as stunning as book one's cover. I couldn't be happier with how it turned out. Thank you.

ABOUT THE AUTHOR

Danielle Hill is an Amazon Top 10 author of drama filled, swoon worthy and magical contemporary fantasy novels. Danielle first came up with the idea for A Kingdom of Sun and Shadow in late 2017 and began publishing chapters on Episode shortly after. After a warm reception on Episode, she decided to expand the story and began writing the manuscript in February 2018. She has already begun work on the sequel to A Kingdom of Sun and Shadow and can't wait to share it with the world.

Danielle resides in a small town in Ontario, Canada and spends her free time creating remarkable worlds full of magic and being a mom to her daughter and dog. She loves Marvel, anime, binge-watching TV shows and cheesy hallmark movie marathons.

CPSIA information can be obtained
at www.ICGtesting.com
Printed in the USA
LVHW101645171122
733396LV00003B/304